SEVEN SINS

BOOK ONE OF THE **SEVEN** SERIES

ARTI MANANI

For my niece, Shreya

You drive me mad, but I love you

I've been told that *Seven Sins* is 'gory', 'brutal' and 'gruesome' at times, so I guess I should probably warn you...

This novel contains strong language and scenes of violence and emotion that may cause offence or could prove disturbing to some readers. It may not be for the faint-hearted. If you don't like blood or gore, I advise that you look away.

And to my friends and family who read this, remember, this is a work of fiction. ☺

Thank you.

Arti

ABOUT THE AUTHOR

Arti Manani is a passionate writer and marketer, born in West London, England. She fell in love with books in her early childhood and wrote her first short story when she was ten, on scrap paper bound together by paper clips.

Arti has come to use real-life situations and experiences, her fears, nightmares, and film as ammunition to create the stories within her thrillers.

Seven Sins is Arti's second novel and the first in the *Seven* series.

Find Arti on Instagram @Author_Arti_Manani
#SevenSins

CHAPTER **ONE**

We are all flames waiting to be fed

Her fierce and angry soul hides amongst the beauty of her light. She's deadly and contagious as she blazes from person to person burning all that she touches. She roams without a shadow and she doesn't want to be seen. She lives in the form of humanity and it's hard to tell. It's hard to tell who is infected with her evil and who is not. Fire, it's a dangerous thing.

Seven days ago

I stood over him and watched as fountains of blood gushed out from where his limbs used to be. He was choking on this thick, dark, molten of red that erupted from his mouth as he glared at me, face filled with cuts and grazes and more of this liquid that streamed down his skin. He watched me as I watched him, burning amongst the lava that poured from his body. It was time to put his torture to an end, he had endured enough.

I leaned towards him, grabbing him by the curls of his hair before dragging what was left of his body through the pool of blood that was seeping from him. He took one final look at his son before I drove my knife into his throat. Blood trickled down his neck as I pushed the cold steel deeper, slicing it open whilst moving it across him as though I were an incompetent butcher. I felt the damage I was causing as the weapon ripped into his skin tearing through his nerves. His groans silenced as I took back my knife. I laid him to rest and waited for the darkness in his eyes to fade before taking a step back to evaluate the mess.

The level of creativity behind this new piece of artwork had exceeded all others. Blood splattered along the walls and ceiling and blanketed the marble floor of this man's living room. It dripped down the corners of the coffee table and spread across the French doors that opened into the garden. Shards of glass were scattered across the room while bits from ornaments and lamps glittered in pools of this dead man's blood.

He had put up a good fight but had still been

defeated. I stood there and watched my creation. My masterpiece. I came out stronger. I did this.

The sound of his baby's cries snapped me out from my paralysis. It was time for me to go and for the cleaners to come. I walked away, wondering what this man had done to deserve this death.

Today

Bad things happen to good people. Take that in for a moment. Inhale it like a cigarette and let it whirl around inside you. This is the kind of thing you hear every day. What does it mean, bad things happen to good people? I wonder. What does one have to do to be crowned a good person? What does it take to be considered a bad one? Who decides what is good and what is bad? Who makes that judgement? Who has that right?

I'm lying here with nothing but my ugly thoughts sprinting through my mind as if running a relay. It's dark in here, here inside my mind and I can't help but ask myself, where did I go wrong? When did I turn bad?

Sometimes my thoughts get the worst of me and I wonder whether I was unfortunate enough to have had an amateur wire up the mechanics of my brain rather than the Man Himself. I wonder whether the same amateur had worked up the story of my entire life. A twisted and sadistic one at that. The kind who'd wave a floating ring at a drowning man. The kind who'd give that man hope but have no intention of saving him. We're playing the devil's game and it's one where hope doesn't belong. You'll see it when it's too late. When you've stepped too close to the fire, when you've been burned by the flame.

Those flames will take away your freedom, your voice and they'll make it theirs. They'll stick a target on your back until you get stung. That sting will turn into a bite, and a bite, a cut. With each strike, those cuts will get deeper. Deep enough to hold the gasoline that they'll pour over you. And then they'll take a step closer until you're a flame. A flame, like them burning in the shadows looking for your next feed.

What do you do to stop a fire from burning? You kill it. You deprive it of oxygen and you suffocate it. Or you let it burn. You let it spread.

Self-defence. That's what it is until your actions become immoral. But what else do you do when the fire keeps burning? When the knives keep piercing? When the bullets keep firing? You allow yourself to get shot or you eliminate the shooter. By then it will be too late because you've made your move. You've committed your sin because you felt the wrath of theirs too many a time. Only this time, you'll make sure you don't get shot again.

You'll surround yourself in armour and you'll leave your guard raised. Protection becomes destruction and it's no longer self-defence. By then you'll be considered a bad person because that's what you become when you look out for you. The darkness will cave in and that's where you'll prefer to be. In the dark, like me. That way you won't get torn. That way you won't bleed.

Except you will, because you're not the only one out there with a weapon. You're not the only one out there protecting your own back. Too many people burned. Too many people scarred.

Am I a flame? I wonder, but I already know. I got too close and now I'm one of them. An angry flame that has spread like a bushfire turning everything in my path to ashes. That's what we'll all be soon. Nothing but ashes. Nothing but dust.

The outcome will be bad for all of humanity because whatever good that is left in this world will slowly disappear. No matter how much good you do, one bad thing is all it takes for you to knock off that halo from your head and replace it with the devil's horns.

How can you tell the difference between the good and the evil when eventually we will all become the same? It's human nature. To kill or be killed. We were supposed to be like this. We were supposed to be bad. Whatever that is.

Two days of confinement is all that it has taken for me to see the reality of what this is. And after forty-eight years of believing I had been doing good, it's taken me two days in this bed to realise that I was just a small flame all along. A small flame waiting to be fed. Just like everybody else.

CHAPTER **TWO**

Do all criminals start this young, or is it just me?

Sugar sprinkles over shame as the chocolate melts down the sides, hiding what's beneath. It's the sweetness of these guilty pleasures, like taking candy from a baby. So wrong, yet so right.

Today

'Morning, Mr Jackson. How are you?'

'Breathing.' I whisper with whatever energy I have. Irene feels sorry for me, I can see it in her eyes but she doesn't know me, she doesn't know what I've done.

She walks into my space uninvited with a bag and I assume she's here to change my catheter. I'm mortified that it's come to this as she holds it up to confirm. She knows. She can tell by the look I'm holding on my face, nothing short of disgust as I close my eyes and pretend it's not happening. This embarrassment, this torture, what man wants this? What man wants his dignity taken away from him? What man wants… Fuck, Irene!

'It's okay, it's okay. I'm sorry, Mr Jackson, let me move that for you.'

What are you doing, Irene? Just move away from here. I don't need my catheter changed, I don't need your assistance and I don't need you to tug on these tubes.

'It's fine.' I mumble in pain, keeping my inner voice imprisoned within me.

'That's better now, isn't it?'

No, it's not. I tighten my eyelids to hide the discomfort that's flowing through me while she continues to tug on the tubes.

'There you go, Mr Jackson.'

She needs to stop calling me that but I don't have the energy to correct her.

The sponges on the soles of her trainers creep to the other side of me and I release the tightness over my eyelids. Her hands feel warm like the summer's sun, unlike the morphine that she's injecting into my veins. They both feel good and I don't remember the last time I'd felt the touch of another human. Human. I wonder if I have the right to call myself that.

'There, all done. I'll be right here if you need anything okay, Mr Jackson?'

She moves to Mr Kahele in the bed beside me as I place myself beneath the shutter of my eyelids and stare into the darkness beneath, allowing my thoughts to get the worst of me.

Does it make me a bad person? Or does it make me human? Maybe I'm just a monster. When your master asks you to gouge out the eye of your next victim to save your family, what do you do? I see them. I see those eyes every night. Blue, green, brown. I don't know their names and I don't know what they did to deserve the torture I was ordered to give them but I see them. The ones who'd put up a fight and the ones who wouldn't. Every time I close my eyes, I see theirs. And for what?

I don't want this wallet. I don't want it. I want my family. My nieces Skye and Bella. I want a spoon full of homemade jam. That's the scent of luxury. That's the scent of riches. I want the aromas of strawberry jam and marmalade dancing up my nostrils with the perfume of fresh bread to spread it over, all whilst being seated at the dining table with Mum, Grace and the twins.

I look at a photo of them through the window

of my wallet. My nieces, they're identical with thick, jet-black hair sweeping off their shoulders, eyes deep blue and bright inside two perfect ovals. Their teeth are white like pearls, beautifully framed by their rose lips. Bella's birthmark drowns within her dimple just like her mother's used to. I imagine this is how Grace would have looked had she lived past the age of twenty-one, but I guess drug abuse can do some fucked up things to people.

I see a lot of her in them. Their faces are long and thin, cheeks protruding more than they should with a shy dusting of pink gently brushed over the peaks of their otherwise pale cheeks. Their noses are sharp and pointy but I don't draw attention to it. I always did wonder whether they'd got it from their father. Never mind.

I close my eyes and wonder why they haven't come to see me yet. The waiting game is making me feel lonely and a little anxious inside.

Discomfort squeezes my chest, remaining loyal to me as it embraces me firmly but it's not the kind of hug I need right now. The blood that had seeped through the thickness of these bandages has dried over but I know what lies beneath is worse. They'll come and change it soon, this bandage, but I don't see the point. I don't see the point in them doing most of the things they're doing for me, but they do. I'd like to think I deserve it, but I know I don't.

Twenty-three years ago

Skye and Bella had dug a hole by an apple tree at the bottom of the garden, filling it with wild berries and bits of grass while taking turns to spit in it. They'd been cooking up a range of dishes, showing off their culinary skills in their purple dresses and matching hair-ties made from Graces' duvet cover.

'Looks like the twins will put Mum's cooking to shame.' I turned to smile at Grace as the gentle sound of her laughter fluttered into the air.

'Doesn't look like we'll be getting any jam for a long time.' Disappointment masked over the softness in her voice as she followed my line of sight and we watched as Mum scrounged for strawberries that weren't there.

'I'll pick some up tomorrow. What else are brothers for?' I winked at her but she looked away.

The colour drained from her skin as she adjusted her curtain of hair, allowing it to fall over her face. I knew my sister, I knew there was something wrong. I knew she was hiding a secret and I knew she wanted to tell me. I should have asked her, I should have tried but I guess I was too busy re-calculating and shuffling around costs in my head so that I would be able to pick up some strawberry jam the next day.

Today

Who knew that the troubles you have when you're young are only a taste of what's to come? Twenty-three years on and I still can't bring myself to forget that day, the last time we were all together. It's shit to think that some of my best memories are the ones I once believed to be some of the worst.

Memories. That's all I have left. Memories of all the good I've done and all the bad too. The kind that brings me regret, making me wonder what it would be like if I had done things differently. If I had pretended to eat Skye and Bella's dinner, if I had helped Mum with the strawberries, and if I had asked Grace what was really happening behind the falseness of her smiles.

But I guess you don't think about those things when you're worrying about your incomings and outgoings not being aligned. When you're worrying about looking like a failure because you can't afford to put strawberry jam on the table for your family. When you've spent almost all of your teenage years dreaming of being a millionaire but life's circumstances have taken you so far away from being able to save even five pounds a month. You do what you have to do and see where it takes you.

What I did landed me here, lying in this bed stuck inside this overly bright room with three other men who are in a similar position to me. Death comes to us all but for the four of us in this room, it will come sooner than we'd like.

I wonder whether these men let society get to them too. It sickens me, all these expectations, all these stereotypes and gender roles that we have to abide by to fulfil the requirements of other people. Because of these expectations, I became greedy. I won't deny what I was. I conducted my life around everyone's expectations of what a man should be. I was supposed to hold up the roof and I was supposed to bring home the jewels. I did what I could for them—my family.

Yet here I am now, wondering where I messed up. Wondering when I became a bad person. A sudden thought creeps into my head and I wonder, maybe I've always been this way.

Twenty-three years ago

'Kai? Hello?' The sharpness of Ethan's voice skewered into my ears, taking me away from my thoughts.

'Oh! Sorry, Ethan, forgive me. I didn't see you there. What can I get you? The usual? A large, soy latte with an extra shot?'

The regulars appreciated the personal experience I gave them every time I remembered their orders, although Ethan was now more a friend, even a father figure than just a regular.

'Please. And this too.' He waved a pot of granola at me before placing it onto the counter.

His hands were as strong as his voice. He was big and tough like an alpha leader in an action film. Tall and hard like a grizzly bear in the wild, but features as soft as the kind of bear you'd gift to a child. When I first met him, I couldn't tell if he was a hero or villain. His hands alone could crush the lives of many and his voice hissed loud enough to shatter souls if he were ever to raise it. But the kindness in his face and his level of politeness told me otherwise.

I turned to the coffee machine as the angry sounds of steamed milk and water pouring from the spouts spilled into my eardrums.

'Anything else, Ethan? No croissant today?'

He waited for the clouds of steam to disappear from the air between us before responding.

'Not today, thanks. I'm trying to cut out croissant's from my diet, so it's just the two, please.'

I nodded, forcing my lips to stretch across my face as the taps of my fingertips against the screen filled the silence.

'You'll be back for sure, give it ten minutes. You've been having croissants with your coffee ever since I've worked here, how long has it been now, seven years?'

'Yes, maybe eight.' He was always so precise. 'I could barely hear you whispering from your side of the counter when you started, and now look at you, you manage this place.'

He looked at me like he was proud but I couldn't look at him. I was a failure to my family, I was a man who couldn't even put a jar of jam on the table.

'Here you go,' I gave him his coffee with another fake smile as the thump of the till crashed into the air singing an unknown melody as the sound of a plastic-wrapped spoon rustled in Ethan's palms. My quiet, sheepish voice whispered in the background shamefully as I held out my arm towards him. 'Enjoy your day.'

'Thanks, son. Stick it in the charity box, will you?' I watched as he trampled towards the exit of the coffee shop with his long, thick, elephant-like legs.

'And don't worry about it, Kai, whatever it is. Although it's the longest thing you'll ever experience, it's also very short. Don't waste your life on worries, okay?'

He walked further away from the counter taking the shrilling sound of his voice with him whilst leaving behind the best advice I have ever ignored.

'See you soon, Ethan,' I raised my voice a little,

trying to imitate his. 'I'll have your croissant ready for you in ten!' I smiled, and from the back of his head, I could tell he was too.

The silence in the coffee shop told me I was alone as I slid the three pounds fifty into my pocket whilst the thickness of my vomit hitch-hiked a ride up my throat.

Today

I guess it was wrong of Ethan to trust me to put his change into the children's charity fund. I guess it was wrong of the coffee shop to assume their employees could be trusted to be left alone. I guess that's where it started. Me standing in the coffee shop when I was twenty-five, stealing from charity so I could pick up some groceries on the way home. The first thing I did that made me a bad person. My first crime. I wonder, do all criminals start so young, or is it just me?

That's already one sin they're judging me on before my life as a criminal had even begun. Criminal. That's what they call me now. Not Skye and Bella though. I wonder why they haven't arrived yet. I look at the time and feel something inside me sink a little. That damn clock is still not working but I reassure myself, there's still time. Surely they'll come.

CHAPTER **THREE**

I don't want to be there when I die

A mirror doesn't give a man a true reflection of who he is. It doesn't show him what's on the inside. It doesn't show him the things he covers up with a smile whilst standing in front of it, telling himself he's okay. Death will. His true form will stand before him, stretched out forming the thickest, darkest queue of truths he's ever seen.

I don't want to be there when I die. Death. Although it comes once, it lasts forever.

Thirteen years ago

The crickets whispering in the thicket of the grass around me told me I wasn't alone. Dirt covered my entire body as I dug deeper into the soil, filling my wounds with the dust that once covered the body of a man who lay here to rest only a few days before.

The damp stench of my sweat surrounded the air as a layer of stickiness covered my body making my jeans and shirt cling on to me tightly. I dug further into the ground with only the light from the moon guiding me as I searched for a needle in a haystack. Each scrape of the shovel took off an inch from my legs making me feel smaller than I already was. Patches of skin tore from my thin, bony hands from over five hours of un-burying and re-burying bodies from the earth. I felt each wound burn with every strike into the dirt as clear liquid oozed from my sores creating a thick, muddy paste that smothered over the palm of my hands with each blow.

I had until sunrise to find him. I had until sunrise to find this one dead body that was hidden amongst a field of hundreds of soulless figures.

I could feel my insides clawing away at me as I scraped the shovel against the dirt, transferring heaps of soil from one end of the grave to the other. The sound of the metal hitting the ground echoed into my ears in tune with my heart as it raced in fear, but the reason for my distress was unknown to me. I couldn't tell whether I was afraid of finding what I was looking for, or the consequences I would face if I didn't. I kept digging, tightening my grip as panic ran through me in desperation to find this body. I held the shovel tight as though holding a machine gun, finger pushed down on the trigger at all times, unable to stop, unable to let go. A sound leaked from the tip of my spade forcing me to shoot that final bullet. The crickets paused with me as they refrained from spilling their secrets into the air. The silence told me that he was there, waiting for me. I felt the bile inside me burn through my stomach as it began to rise from my gut and into my throat. I crouched down closer to him, closer to this pile of meat that was once a human being. I couldn't feel his presence but he was there. A body without a soul.

The coldness in the air wrapped around me tightly as it squeezed onto my guts. The burning sickness filled my mouth as my insides shot out of me as I heaved into the grave of the man I had murdered. I swiped my forearm across my mouth, wiping away the remains of bile that had spilled from me before sliding the dirt away from his face like an untrained archaeologist. The coldness from his skin scraped my fingertips like shards of glass as it hitch-hiked into my nerves, spreading the sharp sensation of ice throughout my entire body as it bit away chunks of my soul.

I found him. His hair was short and black as it

swept back from his pale, blue face. His lips were stained purple as they sat silenced and tight. His brown eyes glistened as they fixated onto mine, staring at me with nothing, telling me nothing except that they were vacant. The moonlight touched his face, secretly showing me what I had taken. This man, he looked like me.

The murmurs of the crickets had filled the air again as they began to whisper to each other about what they'd just witnessed. I found him, but I wasn't done. I wasn't done fulfilling my order. I stood up and continued to dig, faster. They needed this body or at least a part of it, and they needed it soon. I threw the shovel to the side and fell to my knees again as I clawed away, digging into the dirt like a dog looking for a bone. I ploughed into the soil as blotches of red emerged from the palms of my hands.

The crickets paused in silence almost suddenly as the violent vibrations from my phone filled the air. I assumed they had stopped to listen as I kept digging, scratching my nails along the ground below, ignoring the buzzing from my phone whilst the crickets waited. Whilst the crickets waited for me to see what they'd already spotted. I stopped in horror as cold sweat began to drip down my face. My mouth filled with saliva and my insides tangled together, tightening into a large knot. I sat there on my knees and watched as it rested under a thin blanket of soil, almost illuminated by the moonlight. Its colour had disappeared as it lay in a coat of white, drained from the blood that once flowed within it. I found it. I heaved again as I reached inside my back pocket feeling the stiffness down my spine from plentiful hours of vigorous digging.

The sky was preparing above me, getting ready to shed light onto the secrets beneath me. I could see the moon fading slowly through the reflection in my knife. I could see the stars disappear behind a blanket of light that was seeping into the space above me, telling me that time was moving quickly.

I had to do it. I had to do it now. I took a deep breath as I gripped the knife, holding on to it tightly, raising it above my head so the crickets could see before slamming it down and removing the intricate patterns of the access code from this dead man's hand. I wrapped his thumb inside a bag as my mouth filled with saliva and bile. I had nothing left to throw up.

I lit up the grave with my phone as the vibrations continued. Seven missed calls, two voicemails, four messages.

'Uncle Kai, where r u?'

I'm sitting in a grave with a dead man beside me.

'Be home soon. Everything okay, B?'

The three bubbles dancing at the bottom of the screen told me to wait for Bella's reply, but I didn't have time.

I stood up, placing my phone in my pocket as I began to re-bury this man who looked like me.

And then I walked away, out of the thicket of the field knowing that this memory would wander with me for eternity. Knowing that even on the hottest of days, my world would remain ice cold.

'What on earth happened to you?' Skye looked me up and down as my body dripped with filth and sweat.

'Gardening.'

'It's seven in the morning but, okay. I'm going for my run.' She flew past me, exiting the house as if she didn't smell the scent of a dead man lingering over me, as if she didn't hear the screams that were trying to flee from my gut, as if she didn't see the blood that painted my hands.

'Did you pick up my notes from Sadie? They left to go to the airport at six.'

Bella had come running down the stairs in her pyjamas. Her face told me she knew the answer to her question as I stood there and glared at her.

'Uncle Kai, my exam is on Tuesday and Sadie has all my notes.'

I was with Toni and Vin giving them the thumb

that they'd ordered me to cut off. Before that, I'd spent about five or six hours looking for this fucking thumb. And not even nine hours before that, they'd come into work threatening to hurt my family, so no, I didn't drive ten minutes down the road to pick up your notes.

'I'm sorry B, I didn't see your message.'

She looked at me in disgust before starting a stampede on her way up.

I wasn't going to think about how I'd spoiled those girls. Maybe it was a teenage thing, I don't know, I never had a chance to be one.

Five past seven. I was tired but I had to get ready for my morning shift at the coffee shop.

CHAPTER **FOUR**

Maybe I'm just tired

The angels watch from above, looking down into your world from an aerial view. They greet you when you need it most. When they can see you're in trouble and in need of help. But those demons, those demons blow a gentle breeze towards you moving those clouds over you as they steal the light, hiding you beneath the umbrella as you wander blindly under the delicate duvet of the silver cloud. Unseen. Unnoticed. Concealed like a hidden treasure that nobody knows about. The angels can't see you now, but the demons, they can.

Twenty-five years ago

'I love those girls but we were getting by back

then. Before Gracie got pregnant.'

I felt bad. I felt bad each time I heard my thoughts spill from my mouth.

'You know, Kai. You're a good person. You have good values and you take care of your family. Your mum, your sister, those twins. I know it can be hard but you're okay, you'll be okay, Kai.' Ethan moved over to the desserts that were sprawled across the counter.

'You will be okay, Kai.' He whispered beneath his breath and I wondered whether he was telling himself that, or me.

'She fell pregnant when she was just fifteen, Ethan. She dropped out of school and she decided to raise them without the father. I do everything in my power to support them but it's like I've always had a dark cloud over me that happened to become thicker and darker when the twins were born.'

I turned to stare at the doughnuts and cakes with him as my mouth ran like an uncontrollable motor converting my inner thoughts into real, audible words for the first time.

'It's impressive, Kai. You've been here since you were seventeen, yes?' He took a sip from his latte whilst moving his head closer to inspect the carrot cakes that were lined up neatly behind the glass window.

'Yes. So what Ethan? It's not that. It's not about

how long I've been working for. When I was thirteen, it was fine. I was young, it felt good you know. It was nice being able to support Mum, all those odd jobs I did around town all those years ago.' I watched him glide his eyes over to the brownies, confused as though he was having a separate debate with himself.

'It's fine, Ethan. As you said, I'll be okay.' I understand, my problem isn't yours.

Even though we'd both been looking at the same selection of desserts, what we were seeing was different. I moved my head towards the counter and fixated on the coffee stains that decorated it.

'Maybe you need a break, a holiday even. You're probably worn out, Kai. You've been doing a lot from a young age.'

I looked at him in silence but my heart continued to spill in my mind. Yes, Ethan, since I was very young. I was soaring across the sky and I had this scent of masculinity wrapped around me like a warm blanket of clouds and for a while, it was the best feeling. They were happy. For the first time, we could buy luxuries and that was because of me. *I* did this, *I* bought the food to the table because of *my* hard work. Grace had that new jumper because of *me*. Mum was smiling because of *me*. I put shame on all the men who'd walked away from us. Me, a young child, managed to do for my family what they couldn't, and that too before my fourteenth birthday. Do you know how good I felt, Ethan? That *I* made them smile. The money *I* earned. I never knew rich was a feeling until I saw how happy it made Mum and Grace. I could see the impact it had on them. Their smiles. Their appreciation. Their *respect*. Whoever said money never bought happiness was wrong. My money paid for the fireworks that lit up their faces during the darkest of nights. Do you know how much pressure that puts on me? Do you? You know, seeing Mum smile like that all those years ago had set the groundwork of my fixation on money and now all I know is work. I'm desperate to be the first man in my family to do right by them, Ethan. To show them that not all men are unworthy of love. But it's been so much harder to prove since the twins have been around. Does that make sense, Ethan? Does it? But yeah, okay. Maybe I'm just tired. Maybe I do need a holiday. Maybe I can starve my family for a few months so I can use the money to go away for a while.

'Yeah, maybe.' I looked up at him as he took another sip from his latte, eyes still on the desserts.

'I understand, Kai. I'm here whenever you need to talk, okay?'

I'm talking to you now, Ethan. I need your help now. The fog is too much and I can't see where I'm going. I'm falling right into the waters below me and I can't swim.

'I know. Thanks, Ethan. I'm just tired, been a long night, that's all.'

I walked over to sink behind me, picking up a wet cloth before making my way over to the counter again, finding the coffee stains as I scrubbed at the fire inside me.

'You know, I go home sometimes wishing I had a son like you.' He continued to eye up the desserts in front of him but I knew it wasn't the desserts he was seeing.

I wish I was your son too, Ethan. I wouldn't be feeling like this if I had a dad to help me.

'You should call him.' I took a step back to inspect my scrubbing, unsure of how he'd react to my suggestion.

'No.' He stepped back too, away from the cakes as though they'd insulted him. 'We don't speak, you know that. He has lessons to learn. Once he has learned those lessons, he will come back. Until then, he is not my son and I will not speak of him.'

I looked down at my shoes, wondering what his son did that was so bad to receive such tough love from a man as kind as Ethan.

'Kai, I know you work hard. You've got a lot to take care of. I'm here if you need anything, money, or anything, you know that right?'

Yes please, Ethan. We need it. I work three jobs, I have a sister, her two kids and Mum all relying on me to keep it together. I'm struggling. I need support. Yes, please. Ethan, please can you help?

'No, we're fine. Thanks, Ethan.'

Pride or shame? What's the difference?

Today

I'm lying here staring at a clock that refuses to tick wishing my mind could do the same. I can't help but wonder what had been going through my head all these years for me to end up on my deathbed at forty-eight.

I did what I could and I kept going for them. My family. I hope they remember me for that. I hope they remember me for sticking around, for trying.

I can't help but think about my eulogy, it could go either way. My eulogy. I wonder if I'll have one. If I do, I wonder who will turn up to listen.

I squeeze my eyes for a moment because that thought has made me feel a bit shit inside and I fear it's only going to get darker, even with the lights on. But it's not the dark that I'm afraid of. It's the demons that lurk within it. The demons that only I can see when nobody else is there, when I'm alone in the shadows. The kind of demons that I had shut out before, when they were stood in front of me wearing a cape of truth.

I turn my thoughts away from the darkness because sometimes it's easier to pretend I'm not in it. But it's there, even when it's not.

I feel like these wads of notes in my wallet are burning through my fingers, turning into ashes. They're worthless to me now, now that I'm here. The power, the respect, everything I thought it gave me, gone, just like that. I clung on to money the way a devil clings on to his fork, hungrily worshipping it as if it was the answer to my prayers. It may have been, at least for a while but like a pitchfork, the tighter you hold on to it, the deadlier it becomes. And I guess that made me deadly. Because now when I look back through my past, it seems as though this is déjà vu because I died a long time ago. Cremated too because my insides are nothing but dust. I'm hollow. Empty. And the worst thing about it is that I can't tell whether it was murder or suicide.

The devil is playing a beat in my head and I can feel it thumping but I can no longer dance to his tunes. I think I need a top-up, something strong to take this noise away. I don't want to think like this but I've been left here in this room for too long. I feel like I've been imprisoned, incarcerated with a shovel so I can dig my own grave but I won't, not yet. I'll dig deep for sure, deep enough to uncover all of the bullshit from my past so I can lay it out in front of me. I will find out who did this. I will find out how I got here. I will find out who made me bleed. I will remember. I will. I will stay here until the truth stands before me, until I've placed his karma onto him. He is unfinished business that I need to take care of and I refuse to leave until it's done. This grave I'm digging, Patrick, it's for you. I will kill you, even if it's the last thing I do. Your karma will be death by my hands. I will kill you.

The devil inside me has switched up the beat but this time it's in my chest. It's a lot louder and a lot faster and I don't like this new rhythm. I need to stop thinking like this. I can't risk having another panic attack but it's him. The thought of him. He awakens the devil and ignites the fire within me. A burning rage of anger that I must inflict onto him. I need to hurt him, decorate his face with cuts and bruises and take his last breath. I need to kill Patrick.

Happy thoughts, Kai. Happy thoughts. I take small breaths, as agony possesses my body like an evil spirit in his calling. This pain, this pain is too much to bear and I need to stop. I need to stop but my mind, it won't let me. It's never let me. I can feel my chest tighten as the drum echoes throughout my entire body. God, where is Irene?

Come on, Kai. Happy thoughts, don't do this. Don't die.

'Mr Jackson. It's okay.'

I hear Irene's voice and I realise I've set that alarm off again. She's telling me to breathe but I'm struggling. It hurts my chest and ribs and I can't do it. I can't inhale even the slightest. I keep my eyes closed as my hand remains over the wallet that's lying beside me. I can't do anything except wait. Wait to die. Wait to live. I don't know.

CHAPTER **FIVE**

Not everybody looks sad when they are depressed

A beast does not have to be big. He does not need fangs nor fur. He does not need horns nor does he need to howl in the night. He has two eyes, a nose and a mouth. He walks on two legs and he looks just like me.

Twenty-three years ago

I walked home from the grocery store with the weight of a criminal tugging at my conscience. Maybe I was tired from being at work all day, or maybe it was because I'd taken another ten pounds from the charity box. It was becoming a bad habit, an addiction that settled the worries in my head. An easy option to fulfil additional requests, like picking up strawberry jam after work.

'I'm home!' I heard the sound of my voice as it bounced across the empty walls of the front room. Skye and Bella screamed in excitement as they jumped up from the sofa like they did every evening, running towards me to hunt through the grocery bags I had in tow.

'Doughnuts!' Bella embraced me with a tight hug as her little arms wrapped around my legs. 'Thank you, Uncle Kai!' The sweet melody of gratitude sang in my ears as I fed her obsession for sugar.

'What did you get me? Did you get Mum her jam?' Skye continued to rummage through the shopping while I stroked the strands of thick silk that was gliding from the top of Bella's head.

'Oh, yes, I found them! Chocolate muffins.' Skye walked towards me, joining her sister in wrapping her arms around my legs for a brief second.

'Thank you, Uncle Kai.' She yelled as she ran towards the sofa, slumping down as she pierced her teeth into the muffin. Chocolate oozed out spilling onto the purple dress that she'd worn two days in a row.

I peeled Bella off my legs as I moved towards the kitchen sensing an eerie silence in the air.

'Grandma is out and Mum's asleep.'

Even at the age of seven, Bella knew how to read me.

I wondered, for a brief moment, whether Grace was okay. I knew she was suffering from something but I had my own problems to deal with. Maybe that makes me an animal, maybe that makes me a beast, or maybe I'm just human.

'I guess we'd better devour some of those doughnuts and muffins before dinner, what do you say girls?'

'What is devour? Can we eat them now?' Bella's innocent, warm face looked at me, half excited, half confused as we moved towards Skye on the sofa.

'It means we can start enjoying these snacks in three…two…one!'

Bella's smile lit up the room, painting a vibrant splash of happiness across the walls as they both yelled in excitement. I sat there and took a small bite from Skye's muffin as she held it to my mouth. They were happy, they were happy because of that ten pounds I'd taken from the charity fund. Their giggles and smiles had drowned my nausea as my vomit fled to someplace far away. I felt comfortable as I watched Skye coat a thick layer of chocolate over her lips, sticking her tongue out every so often like a snake.

'I'm doing that too, let's put some lipstick on.' Bella dipped her finger into the chocolate of Skye's muffin and smeared it over her lips.

The moment was magical, sitting there watching

two little girls be as happy as they were over the simplest of things bought fireworks to my soul – the nice kind with the colourful waterfalls that crackled into the air, rather than the ones with the loud explosions. But a raincloud began to float in over the sparkles in the room bringing back my nausea as I wished I was able to provide those simple things without having to steal.

'Skye!' I pushed myself away from her but it was too late. The room filled with chuckles of laughter as I sat there, wiping the chocolate from my cheeks.

'I'm going to give you a kiss now too, Uncle Kai!'

And with that, I jumped from the sofa and dug out the jar of jam I'd bought for Grace, hoping it would cheer her up.

'Grace?' I peeked my head around the corner of her bedroom door as the jar of strawberry jam crashed onto the wooden flooring filling her tiny room with shattered glass and thick, red jelly.

She didn't flinch, not even a little and I knew she wasn't asleep. She'd been dowsed with ice water, forever numbed to the world around her whilst her two seven-year-olds guzzled on sugary treats downstairs.

She lay there, pale and pasty with a layer of grey smothered over her skin. Her head was slumped against the drawer like a dead flower as her arms hung limp on her sides. Her cheeks had been stained with tears and I wondered whether she really wanted to die. I fell to my knees watching this body in front of me be nothing but dead.

'Grace?' It was stupid but it was worth a try. 'Grace, stop it.' My voice crackled as I ordered my sister to wake up. 'Grace?' My voice, this time heavier and deeper, echoed through the room as if nothing else was in it. But there was. Grace. Me. 'Grace, wake up.' She wasn't listening.

I could feel myself falling, getting sucked into the ground as though I was sitting in quicksand. I heard my heart thumping faster than the pulse from the clock above her head as sweat seeped from my body drowning me in it's thick, sticky layer of cold heat.

'Grace?' I knew she was no longer there. Everything seemed unreal, more distant and blurry through a lens that was filled with water. The room. The needles. Grace. I sat frozen, lost inside a maze wandering like a dark spec looking for a flicker of light to bring me home, but she was dead.

I stared at her as I placed myself inside my mental coffin. Grace had left me.

'Kai, Grace…'

The sound of Mum's voice ran up the stairs and into my ears as it exploded through me. I couldn't let her come upstairs and see. I couldn't let her world be overcast with the darkest of clouds too. I couldn't let her heart beat cold, I couldn't let her die inside.

'I. We.' My voice crackled again as my throat tightened. 'I… I'm coming.'

I watched her as she slept. I was numbed with her as the sound of the clock continued to tick forwards. I sat there inhaling the smoke that had left her fire as the darkness of this cloud filled my insides with black. I could feel a storm coming from within me as I continued to stare at her, at her arms, the needles, the wires. As I continued to hear the sounds of her children playing downstairs, as I continued to hear this clock that wouldn't stop ticking, as it became louder and louder, screaming at me, beating me with each second, reminding me that time, that time wasn't going to stop even though my world had just ended.

I watched as she slept peacefully while I was there, alive. The black smoke inside me became thicker as it choked the love I had for Grace. She'd permanently removed herself from her motherly duties. She'd used my hard-earned cash and set herself free. She'd left me with her children, her duties, her responsibilities. She'd taken away my ambition knowing true well I'd put those girls before anything else. I sat there watching Grace, lifeless and dead as only those thoughts ran through my mind, going round in circles faster than the wheels of a getaway car.

Except I couldn't get away. I was trapped within the thickness of the forest in a world full of expectations where I had nothing but a devolving society fuelled with unconditional rejection for anyone outside of what was considered normal. She'd left me with the pieces of a broken family and shattered souls. She'd left me to drown in my tears.

I watched her, and I kept watching her. My little sister. Twenty-one, and dead. What would I tell Mum? Her kids? Like all the men in the family, Grace had left us for her own selfish desire to be free without a second thought about the lives of those she was leaving behind. After all her efforts in creating her *We Hate Men Club*, she had made a conscious decision to join them.

I placed my hand on hers, and I felt it. I felt her disappear.

'What's for dinner?'

Mum had been taking chips out of the fryer as baked beans boiled over the stove.

'Grace won't be joining us, she's asleep.'

I took my place and sat at the table, ready to have a meal with the remaining members of my family.

'Come on, Kai, you must take more than that.'

I couldn't. No matter how many chips Mum piled onto my plate, I couldn't eat it. Not with my sister lying dead upstairs.

'You've gone pale, Kai. Is your sister okay? Have you both caught a bug or something?'

'You do look ill, Uncle Kai. You can share more doughnuts with me, it will make you feel better.'

I forced myself to smile at Bella as I sat there at the table feeling hollow and lifeless like a ghost, like Grace. I watched Mum and the twins eat their dinner, clueless to what had happened upstairs. Clueless to what I was going tell them.

Today

I feel a cold sensation surging through my veins like I've been struck by lightning as it infuses electricity into my body. I stare at Irene as she gives me this light that I wish I'd given to Grace.

I see her sneaking in a glance at her watch and I need to know.

'Wha...?' I can't get my words out. It hurts. But the embarrassment on her face tells me that she knows what I want.

'Oh, plenty of time, Mr Jackson. It's just gone four. Don't worry, I'm sure they're on their way.'

She smiles at me sympathetically but I know that

look, that look she gave me, the 'they're not coming, but it's okay, you're not alone,' look. It's the same one I gave the twins when Grace went away. Why would she think they weren't coming? She didn't know them, not even the slightest.

She's got her little washcloth with her and a tub of water and I rather she just shove it down my throat and let me choke to death. I don't feel like a man and I hate it. I hate that I'm spending my last few days being humiliated by these nurses who want to clean me every single day like I deserve to be taken care of. She moves to my sides and runs the cloth along my waist like I'm incapable to do at least that. I raise my arm a little and I feel like a meteor has just shot through my ribs and into my chest. I stop reaching out but those meteors are still shooting through me and there's nothing magical about it. I let her do what she's here to do as I place myself back into the darkness of my eyelids.

Twenty-three years ago

She lay there sleeping inside her final resting place that had been lit up by the sun and I knew where she was heading. We gathered around her like black horses standing over a field of hay with our heads down. Mum's arm touched mine, encouraging me to take the stand as I edged

41

forward, taking out a piece of paper from the inside of my suit jacket.

I allowed my eyes to gaze over at all the faces who had turned up. Our neighbours, Olivia and Harrison stood in the second row behind Mum and the twins, Grace's two friends, Krish and Cate were stood beside them and a few other locals were scattered around the room, including Ms Leeds from the library, Mei from the grocery store, and Ethan the coffee shop regular and the closest thing I've ever had to having a father. I cleared my throat as he nodded at me. I looked over at Mum and the girls, and I took a deep breath.

'It was only the day before Grace had passed when we sat in the garden beneath the cloudless sky. We were watching as Mum searched for strawberries from the planters that hung from the fence whilst Skye and Bella were playing by the apple tree the same way Grace and I used to.

'Grace had accepted a leaf filled with Skye and Bella's delightful cuisine of mud and saliva. She was nice like that. I couldn't take it, even if it was pretend-eating, but she did. She wouldn't hurt anybody. She couldn't.

'I shared a joke with her that day, I won't say what it was but she laughed. She laughed out loud, enough for the birds to flee from the apple tree and fly across the garden. They perched on the roof above us and I assumed they wanted to hear her laugh fill the air again, and I realised then that it had been a long while since we'd seen her that happy.

'But I know now that a smile does not mean that a person is happy, and I guess not everybody looks sad when they are depressed. I should have known. I should have asked. But I guess you can never really know what's going on in someone's head no matter how much they cry, or laugh or smile. It's a dangerous place, inside your head and no one will ever understand it, especially when someone's smiling. And, Gracie? Well, we all know she smiled a lot.

'That's who she was. She'd spread joy putting everyone before herself and she'd shy away from showing anyone her pain because she didn't want to share it. I only wish you did, Gracie.

'Sometimes I think back to when we were younger, and I see her helping me, sticking up for me, fighting my battles. She was my strength. My right arm.'

I choked as I turned the page. Sniffles and shuffling came from the guests in front of me. I looked up at Ethan who nodded again, encouraging me to go on.

'You know, she gave so much, to her friends, her family, her children. She was strong, she was beautiful, and she was always there. Grace was…'

Cries echoed against the high walls of the room putting me on pause as I looked up to see Mum breaking down, clinging on to the girls who both seemed numbed to what was going on.

'Grace was…' I looked back up at Mum but she wouldn't stop. 'Grace…' I stood there and watched. I watched Mum as she tore herself into tiny pieces, shredding her pain onto those girls, those orphans. I couldn't help but blame myself. I took Grace's help but I never offered her mine. I couldn't do it. I couldn't finish. I stumbled to the ground and I cried like a baby. I couldn't finish my sister's eulogy.

'You gave a lovely speech on Sunday, Kai.' Ethan's voice beamed into my ears.

'Thanks for coming.' I whispered over the sound of an angry engine exploding inside the coffee machine as bounced across the walls.

'She was a good kid.'

Ethan looked down at his shoes and I couldn't help but do the same with mine.

'You know, I can't sleep anymore. I'm trying to understand how I missed it.' I continued to stare at the worn leather of my shoes. It was easier to talk that way.

'She disguised her feelings with a smile. She wanted to convince people that she was happy,

Kai.' Ethan's voice radiated into my ears but it wouldn't register. It was my fault. 'Kai, you're not to blame for this. You would never have seen it coming.'

Although he stood on the other side of the counter, I felt as though he'd just hugged me.

'I don't get it. I don't understand how or why Grace could end her life the way she did. No matter what I read, no amount of research is making me understand why she couldn't talk to me.'

I heard myself speak. I heard Ethan speak. I wished I was as strong as he was. I felt my weakness rise above me, sliding out from the box I'd placed it in. I didn't want to continue this conversation.

'Here you go. Large soy latte with an extra shot.'

'I'll take a croissant too please, Kai.'

I looked at him as guilt swiped across his face.

'I won't tell.' I smiled, placing his croissant into a bag.

I followed him out of the shop before locking the door behind him.

I walked over to the fridge clasping my hands onto a jam sandwich before sliding down to the ground. The coldness of the tiles below me numbed my body but my mind was still in full flow. The rustling sound of the wrapper stabbed through my ears as I gently removed the sandwich from its packaging as if performing heart surgery. I allowed my eyes to fill with blackness as I became conscious of the shadows inside me.

'I'll pick some up tomorrow.' You never did get to have your jam sandwich.

Jam seeped out from the sides of the bread as I tightened my fist, squeezing and pressing with all my energy. If I hadn't picked up that jar of strawberry jam after work I would have made it home in time. In time to wipe away her tears and tell her it was okay. But I didn't.

I threw the pieces of bread and jam away from me as it sprinkled over the coffee shop floor. An ocean formed around me as the taste of salt filled my mouth.

'Why, Gracie?' I felt the warmth of my tears glide down my face before stopping onto my lips. What was so bad that you felt you had no other way? We could have fixed things. You could have told me. Why didn't you?

Today

Twenty-three years on and I still ask myself the same questions. I guess soon, I can ask you directly. That's if I'm accepted where you are.

That evening when Grace took her life, she took mine too. I was starved of freedom as I stepped foot in a forest full of poisoned apples growing from its trees. Blood red on the outside, black and rotten on the inside. She'd planted my prison, filled it with deadly thorns and left me to water them every day.

Mum, Skye, Bella. The responsibility was all on me. I needed to focus but my sight had become blurred. I could blame Grace, partly as a reason for why I'm lying here like this today, but I know better. My choices, my actions, my love for those girls. I lost sight, I lost reason, and I fucked up. I chose not to see the truth in fear it would come in the way of fulfilling my goal to be rich enough to support my family, but I know now that money isn't the only form of support that a person needs.

'Mr Jackson.'

I turn to the sound of a sharp, angry voice as it shoots into my ears louder than a bullet. Ivanova nods as she walks across the room, smirking with her nose up in the air like she's royalty. Her shift has just started which means the evening has come.

I wonder whether smug patients and nurses surrounded Mum in her care home. I wonder if she was okay there. I should have asked her. I should have asked her like I should have asked Grace but I didn't and now I've been hit with the inability to speak without discomfort.

The clanging of a metal cart takes me away from my thoughts as Ivanova comes back into my space. I watch as the tray slides off the cart and slams against the hospital floor. The sound fills my ears like a gunshot to my brain but that's not what startles me. She's holding a long, metal pole, thick and rusty, similar to the one that was inserted deeply into my back and pushed out through my chest. She sees me staring at it and quickly turns away to leave. She places it away from my view before running back over to pick up her mess. But it's too late and she knows it. She knows I've seen it and she knows what my mind is doing to me.

It all comes flooding back and I'm back to wondering who it could have been. Who stabbed me in the back with a metal spike and left me alone to die? Which of my enemies would go this far? Who would dare risk facing the wrath of the Crain's? Who wanted me dead knowing they'd have to deal with the likes of them?

Here we go again. Fuck you, Ivanova.

CHAPTER **SIX**

I adapted to the world around me

I don't see the fire, I see colours. Beautiful colours dancing in the dark, waiting to torch the souls of many, charming them with their gentle waves until they magically transform life into the darkness of death, all with nothing but the flickering spark of the dancing flame.

Today

'Morning, Mr Jackson. Can I get you anything?'

Irene sneaks her head into my space, creeping up on me like an animal in the wild. She does it a lot and I can't tell whether she's a tiger or a kitten. I turn my head towards her but a tug around my throat restricts me. I have a tube slithering around my face and into my nose. I look at her, wondering whether or not she's going to explain why I have this cannula on me now and whether she'd just asked a rhetorical question. I'm not able to eat or drink and I have a catheter attached to me. I can't breathe without support and when I talk, it hurts. I give her a cold stare. She knows what I want.

She walks into the thicket of my space gently like a tiger that's focused on the silent sounds of his footsteps, except she fails as her trainers echo against the walls of the room. I can feel it bounce inside the hollowness of my chest and it makes me feel a little nauseous. She has that look on her face and I guess knowing what I want has triggered her sympathetic emotions again.

'You're looking well today.' She purrs at me like a kitten but I'm still not convinced. 'Seems like you had a good sleep.'

She has poor judgement but I also know it's routine. She said the same thing just moments ago to Mr Martinez opposite.

I continue with my cold stare but she doesn't acknowledge this new creature that's wrapped around my face. I could do without this right now. Skye and Bella didn't come yesterday, and Irene creeping into my space as often as she does, with that 'I feel sorry for you' look on her face just reminds me that I'm not worthy of visitors.

'Mr Jackson.' She comes closer and leans towards me so her face is inches from mine.

I can smell her failed attempt to mask the scent of stale cigarette on her clothes through a spritz of flowery perfume and I don't know which is worse. Her yellow teeth are gleaming at me and I'm staring at her, waiting for her to tell me this secret that's shining through her eyes.

'I see on these papers,' she waves a file at me as a layer of gloss sweeps across her eyes. 'I see that it's a little birdie's birthday tomorrow.'

She winks at me and moves away, leaving me to wonder whether kittens kill birds without reason. I say nothing as she smiles and disappears from my view. She put on a pointless show but at least I know what day it is.

'You're looking well today. Seems like you had a good sleep, Mr Kahele.'

I roll my eyes. Dumb routine but she means well.

Tomorrow will be my forty-ninth birthday and I think it will be my first one alone. I hope that Skye and Bella will come and surprise me but I'm not so sure. Hope. I feel myself sink a little into the hollowness of my chest. That word is tragic. I feel like it's bound to me now, now that I'm here. But I can only hope they come because I don't think I've ever been this alone in my head before. I can feel it eating away at me. This loneliness. Like a creature tracing my soul with his cold fingertips, feasting on my veins, digging its claws into my heart, reminding me what it's like to feel.

The word karma strikes through my mind as it tears into the darkness like a flash of lightning. It illuminates the feelings I'd kept in the shadows before it flickers and fades into the darkness. But it's too late and I can see it.

Twenty-two years ago

'Don't feel bad, Kai. You did what you had to do. I'm sure once you're back on your feet you can bring her back. It's only temporary.'

'I know, but I sent her in there without her consent. She's my mum, Ethan.' I spoke down to my shoes, as though Ethan wasn't standing on the other side of the counter.

'How much more can you do? You work here, at the bar, you deliver papers too and you've got the twins. You couldn't look after her. When a parent loses a child it takes a lot out of them. You said she could have put the twins' lives in danger. You did the right thing. She isn't well, Kai. That home is the best place for her right now.'

'I know.' I felt the warmth of the coffee from

the mug in my hands heat my entire body as if I were receiving a hug from Grace, but I knew it wasn't her.

'You should see her.'

'No.' I squeezed onto the mug, forcing the heat to wrap around me some more. 'When we were growing up, Grace and Mum used to have this *We Hate Men Club* because, you know, they hated men. I can't help but put myself in there. Grace is dead and now I can't even look after my own mum.'

'I'm sure she'll understand, Kai.'

'It's okay, Ethan. I need to get back to work now. Thanks for stopping by.'

Today

I wonder if she understood. I wonder if she knew how hard it was out there. How hard it was to look after those girls, and try to live my life too.

Live. I think back to the last time I actually lived and see myself with Grace smiling at me as we eat strawberry jam and bread together. But she's gone, and so has Mum. I wonder if it was that home that killed her. I guess that's on me too.

'Sorry, Mr Jackson. Would you like these open or closed?' Irene pokes her head back into my space and I ignore her.

'Closed it is.'

She removes her head from the gap in the curtain that separates me from Mr Kahele as the sharp squeaks of her trainers move further away. She's becoming irritating but I guess that may be a reflection of me instead of her because I don't know if I deserve this level of kindness.

Like an animal, I adapted to the world around me until it became my norm. This is me now. I'm a killer and I'm yet to kill just one more person. To take his last breath with nothing but the touch of a flickering spark right through his heart.

I can feel my blood heating up but I won't let it boil over. I can't do this. I'd been up most of the night, or at least I think it was night, trying to figure out how I got here, but for the life of me, I can't. I need to think back to everything up until that last moment. I need to remember. I need to know who did this.

I feel my chest tightening again. This oxygen tube. How did it get here? What happened last night? Maybe I did sleep after all.

I close my eyes and hide under a blanket of blackness. It's my favourite place to be. The best way to focus. I feel closer to my soul as I hear the short, shallow bursts of my breath as it tells me that time is moving fast. I have to take myself back, back to when everything began to crumble. I need to know who did this.

CHAPTER **SEVEN**

People look, but they don't see

Friendship. There's something earthy about that word but ships belong in the ocean. I guess all you can do is ride the waves and hope a storm doesn't come. Patrick and I were nothing but paper friends. We were two blank pages that could easily be torn. Yet we didn't tear. Instead, we drowned. He drowned in alcohol, and I in resentment. We were two lost souls each struggling to keep balance, struggling to breathe.

Today

'Mr Jackson!'

I jolt as the sound of Irene's roar strikes me and a sharp, stabbing pain pierces at my chest as though her voice has invaded my insides.

'Oh dear, you look like you're in agony!' She waddles towards me without realising the cause for this sudden and extreme discomfort is her presence.

'Just in time eh, Mr Jackson? I was just coming to top you up.'

She injects morphine into my veins and within moments I feel the coldness gliding through my body. It makes me feel a little more at ease and I wonder whether Grace's drug abuse had the same impact before she overdosed and abandoned us.

'I'm just going to replace your cannula with this, Mr Jackson, it will help you take in more oxygen so you can breathe better.'

I refuse to open my eyes to see what *this* but I can feel her unwrapping this snake from around my face. Thank you, Irene. I open my eyes and she smiles as she replaces the twisted serpent with an oxygen mask.

'You must rest now, Mr Jackson.' She walks away as I relax further into my bed, now with a muzzle around my mouth.

Twenty-two years ago

'Would you like anything else, sir?'

I assumed 'sir' was the most appropriate way to address a man who looked as trim and as sleek as

Patrick did. He was in a smart-looking suit, designer and probably bespoke too by the looks of it. His hair was thick and black like the sands along Iceland's Vik Beach. His jaw-line was strong and perfectly carved like the mysterious fleet of stone figures along Easter Island. His large, round glasses rested uncomfortably on the bridge of his sharp, ridged nose, big and broad, almost as though it was also carved by the Polynesian colonisers of the island.

He pulled out his wallet which housed a thick wad of notes and I allowed for that to be confirmation that 'sir' would be the most fitting way to address this man.

I glanced over at his ID as he took out ten-pounds. Patrick E Healey. Oakham, East London. Born, 1973. He was a few years younger than me. Younger and better off.

'Just this one for now, mate.'

Mate? I had judged too soon. His voice was as sharp as his nose as it beamed over the bar intimidating my softer, quieter tone. He put down the money on the bar instead of handing it to me. They did that a lot, these suited city workers with their gelled hair and shiny shoes. His watch peeked out at me from under his cuff. It wasn't a brand I recognised but I could tell it was out of my salary bracket. I wondered what he did and how much he earned to have so much left over to spend on such items. He smiled, a little smug, as he noticed me looking down at his watch.

'Six o'clock, mate.'

Maybe he wasn't so smug after all. A second wrong judgement made on my behalf. I poured his drink.

'Thank you, sir.'

'Cheers, mate.' He took a swig of his drink and perched on the stool opposite. 'Keep the change.'

It was early into my shift and the night was young but I knew it was going to be a good one.

'You know, you work and you work and you work, and for what? For your boss to call a team meeting to specifically humiliate you and tell you to up your game. Jesus! The economy was crashing, what, three years ago? That's hardly enough time for it to pick back up.'

Patrick had been coming into the bar every evening. I'd only known him for a week but it seemed that was long enough for him to feel comfortable to drown his problems in alcohol and spill his secrets onto me.

'Let me tell you...' He leaned into the bar ushering me to do the same. The stench of alcohol blazed from his mouth and I wondered whether he had been drinking before he came in.

'You see these big bosses, they don't see what I see, do they, my friend?'

I had no idea but I agreed as he handed me an empty glass and nodded at me for a top-up.

Patrick had a lot of bad days. Sometimes I wondered whether he was an alcoholic but I was never sure. The stench of his breath would reek of beer and he always seemed like he was somewhere else. Somewhere hazy in the midst of the fog that frothed inside his head. He was lost. Lost like a soul that had vanished at sea, searching for a place to go except he'd forgotten the feeling of land, the place that had once harboured his being. He didn't know who he was. He didn't know where he was going. He only knew where he had been. It was like looking at my reflection. Except, I wasn't drunk.

'You're what, early twenties?' I was curious to learn more about the well-groomed, wealthy man who kept coming to the bar every evening.

'Twenty-two. Been here since I finished university you know, started as an intern and now, well…' He opened up his arms as if to scream, 'look at me.' And I did, I did look at him. I looked at him and listened as he answered questions that I never asked.

'How about you, mate?'

I didn't want to answer. I guess shame is

something else when you're telling a professional swimmer that you can't swim. He was either going to be my friend and laugh with me, or my enemy and laugh at me. I was about to find out.

'Twenty-six. Graduated three years ago.' He didn't need to say a word. I could see it in his face, and he could see it in mine too.

'Recession.' I'd given him an explanation to my situation in just one word but that sick feeling in my mouth had remained.

Recession, a dead sister, two nieces, care home fees… I was desperate for work. Look at you, what do you know about responsibility? My inner voice got the worst of me sometimes.

'Bummer. But it's something, be grateful.'

I was shocked at his response. He understood. I needed to stop judging this guy. He wasn't too bad.

'Bummer indeed. I'm a paperboy too. Nine to three you'll catch me making coffee at my local café just outside the city, and after six I'm here.' I didn't want to tell him but I needed to show him. I work hard. I'm a fast thinker, fast learner.

'Hey, maybe you could get me into your place?' I looked down at the bar.

'Sure.' He took a long sip from his drink before pushing up his thick glasses that had ridden down his nose. 'I'm sure we'll have something for you.'

I didn't know how to take it but I secretly put

my palms together beneath the bar, thanking God, Grace and whoever else was watching over us.

'Thanks, mate.' I tried to act cool like it was nothing, but I couldn't. It was everything. Grace had been gone nearly a year but I felt her presence through Patrick. She'd come back to me in the form of an angel. But I know now that I'm owned by the devil, as is Patrick.

He handed me his empty glass, nodding at me for a refill.

'Call me Patrick.'

'Kai.' Finally, after one week of speaking to this regular every evening, I was able to befriend him. I took his glass and gave him a refill on the house. That office job in the city, it was getting closer.

'Wait, wait. So you're telling me you haven't tasted alcohol before?' He laughed as he took a swig of his drink. 'But you work in a bar!'

I've never had the luxury to wind down, Patrick. I've never been able to wash away my sorrows in spirits, Patrick. Because I'm haunted by them. It's a different kind of spirit, the kind of spirits that dance like flames in the night. This light, this fire, it follows me, Patrick.

'I don't like it.' I guess sometimes it's easier to keep it simple.

'Mate, if you're coming to that new bar in town,

you're drinking. Otherwise, I'll find someone else to join me.'

I couldn't let him replace me. I needed him to get me into his office. I needed that salary. I walked over to the shelves and grabbed a glass before pouring myself a pint.

Laughter spilled into the air around me as Patrick witnessed me take my first ever sip of this putrid, bitter-tasting drink that somehow made people behave so differently.

He glared at me as I wiped away some of the froth that rested over my lips.

'What's it like, Kai? A party in your mouth?'

More like a funeral. I remained muted as I took another sip of this vile, golden liquid.

'That's it! Let's start tonight after your shift is over.'

A smile crept onto his face as though he were proud of me. It felt good, at least for a while, to *belong*, even if it meant drinking the juices of poison to get there.

'No more, I'm done, I'm done for today.'

'Not bad for your fifth time, Kai. Three pints. Try four next time, toughen up that gut of yours and you'll be drinking like a real man in no time!'

Real man? Please, tell me, Patrick, what makes a real man? Drowning your responsibilities in alcohol every day? Really?

'Yeah, maybe five.' I slurred a little as my eyelids slid and sat halfway down my eyeballs.

Despite the snow that had settled on the window sills, the alcohol promised to keep me warm. Heat sat right at the bottom of my gut as it expelled a tiny spark that fluttered within me. It wasn't a nice feeling and I needed to throw up but I had to hold it together.

'It's okay, mate. I won't tell the boys this time. Go on, let it out, Three Pints.'

You said that last time too, Patrick. Go on, laugh at me, tell your colleagues so you can all laugh at me again. I don't care, Patrick, laugh at me, show me I don't belong. I kept my inner voice muted as I watched him stand from the bench. Finally, it was over.

'Don't mind if I go and pour myself another one do you? Unless you want to get it for me *barman*, you know, in case I break something and your boss finds out you drink her bar dry after hours?'

I don't know what alcohol had against him but it turned him into a shit person, and it made me hate him. The flames within me got stronger and angrier whenever I was around him, giving me a makeover, transforming me into someone I didn't like. Hateful. Spiteful. Maybe jealous too.

Get it yourself, I thought as I got up, stumbling

towards the bar to get him a refill.

'Cheers, mate. Grab me some crisps while you're there, will you? Unless you want to make me a meal too?'

I stumbled back towards him like a clown in a circus, his pint overflowing down one hand and a packet of crisps in the other.

'Unlucky for you, you have to go far to get back home. Can't believe you travel so long just to work in a bar.'

He tore into his packet of crisps as the ruffling sound echoed into my ears. I could hear my heart pumping inside me faster than a rocket being launched into space. I watched him dig into the crisps like an animal that's never seen food before as his glasses escaped from his nose with each bite.

Fuck you, Patrick. Got your ego boost, have you? Your clothes, your job, your car and your new apartment in the city. Want to remind me of anything else I don't have?

If only I had a voice to give him a piece of my mind. If only I could bite back as hard as he bit me. As hard as he would bite me every time we'd drink together. But I didn't. I didn't have a voice. I was muted.

'Yeah, pretty unlucky.'

I was fueled with hate, with anger as it whirled inside my mind. I had silent conversations with myself. Three pints had led my thoughts astray and I realised I shouldn't have agreed to drink. I guess it was envy, another sin committed before my acts of crime. But it is what it is.

Today

'You're not asleep? Mr Jackson, you need to rest.'

Irene doesn't need to be here. I wonder if she's checking in to see if I'm dead yet. Do they need more beds? Is that what it is? She gives me that look and reminds me again that Skye and Bella haven't arrived.

Irene's still standing by the curtain looking at me and I sense that this is not one of her usual rounds.

'You mind if I share my lunch-break with you, Mr Jackson?'

She strides in and takes a seat on the chair beside me and I wonder if she knows something I don't. Is this how I'm going to go? With Irene sitting beside me out of sympathy? This is not my karma. I don't deserve to go like this.

'Don't worry, you have time. I just thought you may like some company, that's all.'

She reads me well. Her accent seems a lot stronger now but I can't tell where she's from. I think she feels relaxed with me, but I can see she's already bored and I don't blame her. I'd like for her to leave too but she's sitting here with a newspaper in her hands and I can't help but wonder if my face is in there, under 'Missing' or 'Wanted'. There's a big difference. The life or death kind of difference.

I begin to raise my arm towards the clock.

'It's two-thirty, Mr Jackson.' She smiles at me as she sits back and opens up the paper.

'Kh,' I try to speak as the sound echoes in my muzzle and I wonder if she heard me. Her eyes peep over the side of the paper to look at me.

'It's two-thirty, *Kai*,' a smile slides onto her face again before it hides behind the newspaper.

Thank God, she's just here to sit and read. I allow the darkness to creep in over my eyes. I should probably sleep while Irene is sitting here, or at least pretend to sleep before she starts speaking. She doesn't seem to know how to read people. Or she does. I don't know. I don't know if I need her company but her being here makes me feel a little at peace and I guess I could rest my eyes a little.

Twenty-one years ago

'It is easy for me to see *who* a person is by looking in their eyes. I've spent my whole childhood observing people, seeing the devil in their souls.' A smile crept across Patrick's face as he took another swig of his beer before wiping the drool from his mouth. 'People look, but don't see. I see. I see things and I feel things that most normal people usually don't. I go deeper than an empath and it's pretty disgusting, some of the things I see and some of the things I feel. So don't judge me when you find out things about me. I try to be as human as you, but I'm not.'

'Who is?' I didn't know what he was talking about but his eyes were glazed over with a thick layer of darkness and I knew I wouldn't get through.

We'd gone further into the city where the drinks were a lot stronger. The bar was filled with party-goers drowning their souls in spirits late into the night. Patrick was slurring and swaying on his seat as he spoke to me with a cold stare piercing through his pupils towards a group of girls.

'Come on, let's call it a night. It's getting late.' I was ready to leave.

'You see these girls? Pick one.' His voice boomed to the sound of the music that stormed out the speakers behind me, crashing into my body with every beat.

'I can take any. Even if she doesn't want to.'

I didn't know if I was hearing correctly. The alcohol, the loud music, it had all gotten to me.

'Whether she likes it or not, I can.' He laughed

and I knew that last 'one more drink' should never have happened.

'Want to know a secret?' He moved in close to me, closer than I would have liked, enough for me to taste the beer from his breath as he spoke.

'They ask for it. Like her, look over there.' He pointed at two girls seated by the window, one of them looked over and smiled and he smiled back.

'She's seen my suit, my shoes, my wallet. She knows what I'm worth. I'll go over and talk to her, and she'll flirt, and then we'll go somewhere private. They're all the same.' He came in closer as I felt his lip brush against the hairs of my ear.

'There's not one thing that money can't buy, Kai. It'll silence her.'

He wiped his spit from his mouth and moved back proudly to take in my reaction. His face became blurry and I heard nothing but his heavy breath over the music that had now become an inaudible drone pumping in the background. I paused while I waited motionless as my thoughts caught up to me. His words pushed me six feet to the ground, knocking my senses back into me.

'Go home, my friend. Your night is over. Mine has just begun.' And with that, he walked off.

I realised then that I had befriended a rapist, but I needed that job.

CHAPTER **EIGHT**

One word is all it takes to destroy the kindness

Go back to when it happened. Go back. Go back to the most painful memory of your life and relive it again and again, every single day. When you wake up, when you sleep. Live that memory. Deep and horrible. Live those traumas of the past. Hear those words. Feel that sting. Stare hard into the looking glass, grab it and hold it tight. So tight until it slices at your skin.

If someone else fails at doing it for us, we do it to ourselves. Humans. We self-destruct.

Today

I wake up to Ivanova standing beside me as she injects more painkillers into my veins.

'Give me a moment, Mr Jackson, I'll replace that.'

She points somewhere by my side towards my catheter. I assume it's full.

'You're still filling up.' She looks at a large tube, filled with mucus that's being drained from my lungs.

I don't see the need for your assistance, especially when we both know I'm leaving in a body bag, Ivanova. Just leave it, I think to myself, but I say nothing.

My throat is dry and lumpy and I wonder if my voice-box still works. I want to clear my throat from what feels like the ashes of those I've killed as they cling on to the insides of my windpipe trying to steal molecules of air from reaching my lungs.

I slept well but the lids of my eyes have decided to force themselves closed and I wonder whether Ivanova has given me a sedative instead of morphine. Either way, it feels good. She cleans up after herself and walks away, I assume, with her nose still in the air as she sniffs out her next patient.

Twenty-one years ago

It was like working at a theme park, watching everyone else enjoying themselves over the thrills of the rides that they'd spend hours waiting in line for.

At the bar, they'd queue up to be served a pint of happiness that they'd intoxicate themselves in, allowing the alcohol to take them on their own rollercoaster ride while I watched. Watched and served.

Patrick and a crowd of other men in similar dress code to him were sitting at the larger table near the back, cheering and laughing as though they were preparing to jump onto a rollercoaster.

'Kai, can you deal with it?' My boss nodded her head towards them as she walked to the exit.

I nodded back, knowing I couldn't. She turned to leave for lunch, abandoning me in the cage with Patrick and the rest of his wild animals.

'Guys, guys, this is Kai.' The distance in his eyes told me that he'd already had too much to drink.

'He's twenty-seven, graduated with an economics degree.' He stumbled as he moved to stand, before throwing his hand on my shoulder, using me to keep his balance.

'For those of you who don't know Kai, he works right here.' Patrick slammed his hand on my back as his colleagues smiled. I stood there and watched as a layer of arrogance blanketed each of their faces.

'We'll have the same again if you don't mind.' He sat back down feeling proud of himself as I moved away from the smirks and giggles that pierced through my ears.

'He's the one I was telling you about. He tried poaching me for Mike's role. This guy, a bartender.'

I may have been blinded by his friendship, but I wasn't deaf.

'You can't kick someone like that.' 'He's not spineless.' 'He doesn't smell!' 'Don't hit him!' 'Pick on someone your own size.' 'Leave him alone.'

Every school day would be the same. Every single day. Grace would step up to the bullies and she always had my back.

'When you don't have a voice, you can't stand up for yourself. You need to speak out, Kai, show them you're strong.'

She was right but I didn't have a voice. I could see them pointing and laughing at me, laughing that my little sister had to fight my battles. I made myself a target for everyone around me. I was the weakest person in the playground and I fell prey to the other kids who were bullied too. It's a natural process, one I struggled with, a tactic that everyone used to make sure the focus was on somebody else. I couldn't move the focus on anyone, I didn't know how to. So I took it. I let them build their ego, to make themselves feel stronger. I let them change the direction of attention onto me so that no one would notice their scars, like no one noticed mine. No one but Grace.

'Fight back, Kai.'

'I can't. There's something wrong with me.'

And she'd hug me until the tears stopped rolling down my face.

I walked away from the bar feeling that same emptiness as I did when I was at school. Except this time Grace wasn't there to walk with me. I wish I had stuck up for myself. I wish I knew how. But the only fights I ever had were the ones inside my head. And I'd lose those too.

I felt it all over again, and I could feel myself burning up as I walked back to the bar as their laughter sliced at my eardrums. A fire had ignited inside me turning my insides into ashes as it began to burn away the goodness that once resided there.

You don't need to be violent to be a bully. One word is all it takes to destroy the kindness within the soul. One word is all it takes for you to remove your halo and smash it into pieces so fine that not even a miracle would be able to put it together. This man, this rapist of a man who had too much pride and no dignity or respect had humiliated and belittled me. He came into *my* space and made *me* the fool.

I was a good person. I worked hard and did right by my family. How did someone like Patrick deserve to live a luxurious life after what he had done? He wasn't a good person. His actions didn't warrant his trophies and they certainly didn't justify his happiness. I hated him. I hated him and everyone else who spoke to me like I didn't matter.

I feared I was coming close to reaching my breaking point. That thing we're taught, about sticks and stones, how names won't hurt, it's true. It doesn't hurt, because it fucking kills. And if I knew how to fight, I'd make sure I'd use those words to kill Patrick.

CHAPTER **NINE**

If there was anything darker than black, it was me

Revenge. There's something bitter about that word, but it's sweet. So, so sweet.

Today

I open my eyes feeling a layer of hate sticking to the clamminess of my sweat. I can feel myself panicking, or at least I think I am. I'm breathing but the air won't go in and I think my lungs may have been stolen from me. I feel like I have an invisible noose around my neck and it's only getting tighter. Is it me? Am I doing this to myself? I wonder if this is my time and realise I may not make it. I may not see the twins.

'Mr Jackson, come on now.'

Ivanova walks in as though I've distracted her and I can't help but feel a little guilty inside. A deadly silence creeps into the room as she turns off the beeping sound that I hadn't noticed was going off to begin with. A sudden spray of air bursts through the oxygen tubes and into my mask as she stands beside me like a guard, telling me to take deep breaths. She's panicking and it's making me panic too.

'Come on, Mr Jackson, breathe for me.' The look on her face contradicts the calmness in her voice and now I'm fucking scared.

I can't take deep breaths, Ivanova, I can't take deep breaths. My chest is caving in. I want to tell her but I'm muted from the pain. She's lowered herself towards me, breathing deeply and I attempt to breathe in tune with hers but the short and sudden puffs that leave my mouth tell me we're out of sync. The pain that's striking through me like continuous flashes of lightning burns through my lungs, forming a layer of burnt holes and it's making it harder to breathe. Another nurse runs into my space, shouting that my mask isn't strong enough as she tops me up on more painkillers.

'I won't be long, Mr Jackson.' Ivanova leaves my space and the other nurse follows behind her, leaving this storm to form inside my chest.

I need to hold out for the girls for at least one

more day but I can feel the whirlwind inside me, taking the oxygen from within my lungs, moving like a twister as it eats up every inch of air that I have. I open my mouth as wide as my muzzle will let me, trying to gulp down the air but it won't go in. I need to see them. I need to see the girls.

'Here we are, Mr Jackson.'

Ivanova rushes back in with a large plastic triangle in her hand with a larger, thicker tube coming out of it.

'This is a stronger oxygen mask, Mr Jackson, to help you breathe better. I'm just going to replace the one you have on now with this. Try and take deep breaths for me.'

I can't, Ivanova, do not take this oxygen away from me, please. I can feel the fear erupt from within me and from the look on her face, I know she can feel it too as it spills onto her.

'This might feel uncomfortable, there's going to be a lot of oxygen being pushed through into your mouth and nose to help you breathe, okay?'

She talks to me like I'm a baby as she places the mask over my entire face. I feel like I'm drowning in a box and I don't like it. It's so fucking tight. This air is blowing at me and it's making too much noise. I feel like I've been thrown down a wind-tunnel and the only way to stop it is to land flat on my face at the bottom.

'This will help you breathe more comfortably. You're not getting enough oxygen flowing through your body so this new mask will help. Deep breaths for me, okay? I know, it's not going to feel nice, Mr Jackson.'

Who talks to criminals like this? I am a grown man, one who has done a lot of bad things in my lifetime. This Ivanova, she is very patronising. She doesn't know who I am and what I'm capable of doing. A sudden coldness runs through me as she tops up my morphine and I realise I'm not capable of doing anything anymore.

'I'll come back soon, okay, Mr Jackson?'

She leaves my space, still with that smug look on her face and I wonder whether this act of hers makes her feel powerful.

Twenty-one years ago

'Whisky on the rocks.'

A tall man stood on the other side of the bar as he slid a twenty-pound note towards me.

'And another for my friend.'

Another man came in through the doors and took a seat on the stool beside him.

Toni and Vin. They were nice when I met them. I guess I didn't learn anything from my first experience in befriending a stranger at the bar.

'Get one for yourself too, you look like you need one.'

Toni put another twenty on the bar as the crowd of animals roared in the background.

I didn't drink whisky, but I didn't care. The feelings from my past had resurfaced because of Patrick's remarks. I needed a drink.

'Loud bunch.' Toni turned to Patrick and his crowd as they continued to howl and cheer.

'Yeah, they think they're some real big-shots just because they work at the biggest property exchange market in the country.'

Toni and Vin had turned to each other and smirked, but I was too busy hating to take notice. Vin turned to me, taking a quick glance at my nametag before leaning further into the bar.

'Kai, can I call you Kai?' Vin's voice was as smooth as the baldness of his head. He was large and round and I wondered whether he was a security guard at one of the nearby buildings, or bouncer. But when I looked into his face I knew it was something worse. His suit wasn't pinstriped and he didn't have a cigar hanging from the side of his mouth but something about him screamed at me as I pictured myself serving whisky to the sons of Don Corleone. His actions, both of theirs, were different to most. There was something serious about them that meant business. Real business.

I nodded, feeling more grounded to my surroundings.

'You know those guys, do you? You speak to them?' Vin was interested and I could tell from the two fifty pound notes coming out from his pocket that I was into money.

'Not really. One of them used to be a friend of mine.' I poured myself another drink and refilled their glasses.

'And by *the biggest property exchange market in the country,* you mean the Rise Estate of London?' Toni leaned in.

'Yes, they're all employed by R.E.L.' They seemed interested and I was also becoming more willing to help out as Vin slid the two fifties across the bar towards me.

'What time does your shift end, Kai? We'd like to discuss some important matters with you.' The notes teased me as they peeked out a little from beneath his hand.

'Midnight.' I knew I was in.

That anger receded a little from within me when I saw a hundred pounds looking at me. Two pinks earned within a two-minute conversation. I wasn't to know the situation I was about to get myself into. I didn't know who they were. Even if they had told me they were members of the Crain Family, it wouldn't have made a difference. They weren't known to me. I wasn't from the city.

'I wouldn't mess with them, Kai.' Patrick wobbled slightly as he stretched his arm to put his card into the machine. 'Those guys who were in here before, I saw you talking to them. I wouldn't.' He jabbed his fingers at the machine.

'You're not me.' I stared him in the eyes as I peeled his receipt from the card machine. 'Sir.' I placed it onto the bar between us before moving on to the next customer. Fuck him.

'No hard feelings about before, mate. It's all just fun and games.'

To you maybe. For me, it's personal. It's mental abuse. I had let that shit take away my childhood and there was no way I was going to let it take me as an adult.

I wanted to know what Toni and Vin had in mind. Whatever sinister plan they had, I wanted in on it even more now that Patrick had warned me off. Revenge would be sweet and I knew it would be something to do with R.E.L – Patrick's place of employment.

The eeriness of the empty bar made me feel vulnerable as I sat with these two, large men at the table, sipping on whisky.

'For us to carry out this job, you must befriend

Patrick Healey. You must not disobey us, and you must remain loyal to the Crain Family. When you remain loyal to us, we will remain loyal to you.'

I wasn't so sure I'd made the right decision anymore. The bar was dark and with every word I heard Toni speak, a little more darkness managed to creep in.

'You will be paid, Kai. Your family will be taken care of. We need information on R.E.L and we believe that you may be the man to do the job.'

I understood. They wanted me to get Patrick to leak out information to help with their scam, or whatever it was they were embarking on. Simple. I relaxed my shoulders realising it wasn't as bad as I thought it was going to be.

'This isn't a small project that will run over a few months. This is years of planning. Years of information. You need to be with us over a long period. He needs to trust you for you to obtain the facts.' Toni looked at me.

I hesitated at the thought of being friends with a rapist for such a long time, especially as the guardian to two young girls.

'You will be paid generously.' They each stood up and put on their coats.

'Text me when you're ready.' Vin reached out his hand for mine, magically placing his card into the palms of my hands. He was strong. Very strong.

I locked the doors behind them and poured myself another glass of whisky. I felt as bitter as the liquor I was drinking as I realised that my morals had been the only thing stopping me from meeting my lifetime goal to be rich.

This business with them meant money. Real money, but it was earned by doing wrong. But where did doing right get me? It was too easy a decision to make but I had two little lives at stake that kept telling me otherwise. Skye and Bella were ten. I couldn't risk having Patrick anywhere near them. I continued to pour whisky into my glass. I didn't even drink whisky.

'This guy, a bartender!' I could hear his voice over and over as his friends laughed at me. It was never funny. Not at school and not at the bar.

I moved back over to where I was seated before with Toni and Vin. They'd left me a little gift. Another two pinks. I knew I was being bribed but that was two hundred pounds they'd given me in total, for spending less than thirty minutes with them. I had a lot to think about.

Today

I lay here now and wonder what it was that made me do it. I can't decide whether it was money or revenge. Did my history of always being a target lead me to become a monster?

I know now that it wasn't just because of my love for those girls. At the time it made sense, it made sense to take the opportunity of giving them everything I never had growing up. I owed it to Grace. I owed it to Grace to give her children a better life. Yet I think it may be more than that. Maybe it was revenge, maybe it was to show everyone who looked down on me, who used me, that I had risen from the grave that they put me in. That I had risen, not to fight back, but to be someone. I don't know why. Maybe it was just a way of sending out a big 'fuck you' to all of those who screwed me over.

Twenty-one years ago

I sat at the table, drinking whisky after whisky trying to make the right decision. The liquor got me thinking back to all of the nasty memories of my past and I could feel the volcano erupt inside me as fear ran up and down my spine, into my toes and fingertips as I began to lose control.

My hands trembled as I questioned my motive in my head, wondering why I wanted to hurt those around me so badly, wondering why I wanted to hurt Patrick so badly. I needed to talk to someone. I needed reassurance that it was going to be okay, that I wasn't losing my mind. I searched for Ethan's number in my phone.

'Ethan? Ethan?' I could hear the sound of my voice as I slurred into the microphone.

'Ethan, I think I'm about to agree to do something bad and I'm scared. They're making me turn bad, Ethan, everyone around me. They know I can't defend myself, I know it.' I swayed on the edge of my seat as I continued to spit my words into the phone.

'Why do all these people treat me differently? I hate these people, Ethan. They're making me turn bad.'

Saliva shot out from my mouth as I confessed my inner thoughts from my childhood into Ethan's ears as though he was a priest, yet I wasn't asking for forgiveness. I spilled my secrets aloud, telling him of the truth about how I felt, about those who'd bury me, killing the goodness with their words and actions. I could feel my gut fill with hatred towards all of those people as the roars of the fire within me refused to extinguish itself.

'Just because I'm muted, it doesn't mean I can't feel, Ethan. Help me, please, before I do something bad.'

Hearing my thoughts out loud for the first time made me feel at ease and I was grateful for Ethan's presence. But he said nothing. The sound of his continued silence began to sicken me as I came to the realisation that this man and I weren't as close as I thought we were. He didn't care. His silence proved it. I wiped my sleeve across my mouth, clearing away the spit and saliva that drew from it as regret planted itself inside me, growing thick and fast, entwining around my words as though they meant nothing. As though I hadn't been crying for help. As Ethan sat on the other end of the phone, holding a floating ring as he listened to me drown in my burdens. I placed the phone onto the table and gulped down the remainder of whisky from my glass, appreciating that I had failed to hit the dial button. I had been talking to myself.

I sat there as I slumped my head down onto the stickiness of the table, weighing out the pros and cons of my next move. Teaming up with Toni and Vin meant being stronger than Patrick. I wanted to, but my weakness was my kindness and I still had some left.

Although some of the things he did weren't humane, Patrick was still human. I couldn't do that to someone. I wasn't that person. The same way I never hit back at those bullies at school, I decided not to take revenge on Patrick. I wasn't going to release a lifetime of locked-up feelings onto one person. I wasn't going to stoop low enough to become worse than those who acted maliciously towards me. I was going to walk away, from Patrick, Toni and Vin. I was better than that.

'You can only do what you can, Kai. As long as you do good.'

I could hear Ethan's voice sing into my ears, advising me as I pictured us standing in the coffee shop. I saw him, strong and powerful yet calm and composed. That's who I wanted to be. I wanted to be Ethan. Not Toni, not Vin.

But I fucked up.

I stared out of the window, dazed and drunk as I forced myself to stay awake in fear of missing my stop. The bus's speakers hadn't been working and it was hard to know where I was. The light from the lampposts outside stretched across the windows and I struggled to see through the light and into the darkness.

I wobbled slightly as I stood up, holding on to the pole as I struggled to get my phone from my back pocket.

Patrick? At this time? I swiped to answer.

'Kai, I screwed up. I need your help. If anyone asks, I was with you at the bar until, what's the time? Now. I was with you until around two in the morning, okay? Fuck, I thought she was drunk. Kai, she knows my face and she doesn't want my money. My word against hers right? I was with you if anyone asks.'

He was panicking.

'You want an alibi?' Words slurred from my mouth and into the phone.

'You drunk?' Hesitation rung loud in Patrick's voice.

'Am *I* drunk? Sir Patrick is asking if *I'm* drunk. Damn, I guess I am.'

'Kai, I'm serious.'

'Okay, okay. You were with me. Sir Patrick was with Kai Jackson.' And just like that, I had made my choice.

I hung up and sat there staring at my screen as I felt the dead weights at the ends of my fingertips type the word READY into my phone before preparing to release the darkness that lived in me.

A lifetime of rage and disappointment arose from within me and my heart hardened like concrete. I don't know whether I was numbed by the whisky but I felt alive. I felt my cage shatter to pieces and I knew, I knew I was free. Free to live in the other world that was inside me. The darker world where I was finally able to look out for me.

I was going to be a part of the pack of predators. The kind I used to hide from. There was more than one devil and I was about to become one of them. I had my red cape and my pointy horns and was ready to use them to pierce any man that would try to destroy me. In the name of the Crain Family, I was given the flame and it was time to play. For us devils, we love to play with fire.

Patrick was going to get what he deserved, the Crains were going to drop him from his high-chair and he would be left worse off than me. There was no turning back. The fire had ignited as my soul filled with thick clouds of smoke. If there was anything darker than black, it was me.

I hit send.

I thought acting on anger was bad enough, but acting on excessive alcohol intake has proven to be just as worse. I guess that's why gluttony is also a sin.

CHAPTER **TEN**

It was only dark

He's as dark as a demon, as negative as a journalist's library of photographs waiting to be developed. He shakes his head at me and he tells me no. He feeds me poisoned apples and he stands with me in the form of a black shadow.

But the other one, the other one sitting at the table of my mind, he is scared. He is afraid and he is choking. He is weak and lost. He has no shadows and he leaves me to stand alone.

I have to pick one. Do I stand alone in the darkness, or do I rise in the shadows? The choice is mine, but what they fail to tell me, is that it doesn't make a difference. Either way, I am destined for destruction.

Nineteen years ago

I stared into the rearview mirror and felt my entire body shut down for a brief moment. Disbelief struck my soul upon seeing the two men sitting in the back of the Maserati, soaked in sweat and blood. The cold stares in their eyes told me to concentrate on the road as I moved forward, keeping my mind focused on the two killers behind me. I tried to tell myself it was a quick pick up and drop off but I couldn't hear myself think through the silence that screamed its way around the car.

'Stop!' One of the men behind me raised his voice. I felt my arms tremble as I stuck the vehicle in reverse, slowly edging it back to where I should have dropped them off.

He'd broken the rule. He commanded me to stop, communicating with his driver. We weren't allowed to speak. I moved my foot onto the break as I wondered whose fate it was to see their insides first.

'Ah, my final latte from Kai Jackson.'

He took a sip from his large, paper cup, leaning onto the counter, waiting for me to finish serving my last customer.

'After all these years, you're doing it, you're leaving. I'm proud of you, Kai.'

Thank you, Ethan. Thank you for being such a good role model. Thank you for being so polite despite your riches, despite your status. Thank you for being different from the rest. You're a good man, Ethan.

'Thank you. And thank you for popping by before the end of my shift.' I walked over to him, giving him a croissant for the last time.

'Don't forget to live, Kai.'

Oh, Ethan. You're so naïve. I work with the Crains now. I can live a thousand times on this salary. I don't need to work these hours anymore, I don't need to work here anymore.

'I won't.'

Today

'Evening, Mr Jackson.'

Ivanova is back. I do nothing to acknowledge her. I'm tired and I don't want company. At least not from her. Something about her gives me the creeps and she always has a look in her eyes as if she knows something. I wonder why she bothers to waste her time on me. Ivanova, have you been assigned to work with the Crains?

She walks up to the machine to check my oxygen levels and heads over to write something down on the clipboard that's hanging at the end of my bed. I can feel something strange leaking from the energy she's giving off but I'm not sure and I wonder if I'm just being paranoid. I've seen things like this before, I know what happens to people when they're low on oxygen. They start to feel and experience strange things, they get hallucinations and see weird shit. I wonder if my oxygen levels are too low. Ivanova is my nurse and she's only here to help me. She has not been employed by the Crains. I tell myself that but I'm not so sure.

'Resting up I see.'

She's in a good mood and I assume she's got her first paycheck from the Crains. I'm doing it again. I can't help but suspect everyone. I don't like that she keeps interrupting me every so often. She's disturbing my peace, or at least what I have left of it. The keys in her pocket clang each time she takes a step and the soles of her trainers squeak against the polished flooring like Irene's. She walks with her nose up in the air and she acts all smug. But, no. I need to stop. She's here to help me. That's all.

'It's eight-thirty, Mr Jackson.' She walks out of my space and I feel a sensation of heat rush through my entire body. It feels as though the hairs over my arms have become as sharp and erect like the prickles of a cactus plant. Did she make that remark out of spite? Are they keeping the twins from visiting me? Why did she remind me they haven't come? Why does she did think I haven't noticed that already?

Although it's too late for them to come today, I know they'll be here tomorrow. They've never missed my birthday. I have hope.

'Evening, Mr Kahele. Resting up I see.' I roll my eyes. They're all the same.

Chasing money transformed my life, but not in the way it should have. I was living on the mountain of success as my pockets overflowed like a boiling kettle filled to the rim. I was comfortable at the top of the tree. I was no longer disadvantaged or deprived as I had been before. I was amongst the clouds looking out to the world through a different lens. I chose society's version of success without considering my own. Life. Health. It wasn't on my agenda. Money kept me warm and I chose to walk up the paper mountain accompanied by bleeding souls and disrupted spirits. There was no time for health and nature, except when I would stop and take a bite of the forbidden fruits along the way.

The energy I had on my way up this sinking mountain was fueled by the errands I'd run for Toni and Vin, collecting money and driving them around all whilst keeping on top of my bigger role in befriending Patrick. It was just the beginning. It wasn't what I signed up for, being an errand boy in my mid-twenties to early thirties, but the extent of what I did agree to was much worse, as I later found out.

Sixteen years ago

'Can I get you a coffee or anything? I mean, it won't be the same as it was in the coffee shop.' I hovered around the living room wondering what it was that bought Ethan to my home.

'Kai, I don't know how to say this so I'll say it the once and then I will leave.'

He sat on the sofa, tall and large with his elephant-sized legs folded in front of him.

'I've seen you hanging around those two men, Kai. You don't want to get involved with them.'

I felt the blood drain from my face as Ethan's words pierced into me. How did he know who they were?

'I won't ask you why. I'm just telling you, you don't want to do that.'

I don't know why, Ethan. I don't know if it was greed that led me to them, or revenge, or was it meeting expectations? Or wanting to give what I could to my family? I don't know.

'What are you talking about?'

'I've seen you. I know what you've gone through

but working with them isn't the way. This line of business, it shouldn't be on your plate. You know if you need a job you can work at my firm, you just need to say the words and I'll help you, Kai.'

Ethan glared into my soul as I looked down onto the carpet beneath my feet, into the hells below me.

It's too late, Ethan. I'm with them now. My past and everything in it, maybe all of those things were the ingredients to the dish I've been served by the Crains. It's too late, Ethan, I've already agreed.

'I appreciate your concern Ethan, but it's fine. You should leave now.'

He remained seated as I stood there. Frozen.

'Too much power can cause destruction, Kai. I've seen it before. It's a vicious addiction to have.'

He was right. Working with the Crains gave me power, the power of money and strength.

'The Crain Family, they're one of London's most dangerous families. Although they aren't the likes of the Kray Twins, their tactics aren't too far off, Kai. Unfortunately, I have crossed their path before.'

'How do they get away with everything?' I moved to the sofa beside his and sat down.

'The Crains have an arrangement in place with members from the local authorities. It's a mutual understanding of injustice based on nothing but bribery and corruption shared amongst the right kind of people – the wrong ones. As long as they don't leave a mess behind, they won't get caught. Everything done under the name of the Crain Family is overlooked.'

It's fine, Ethan. What I'm involved in is only a small injection compared to all of the other, larger operations that they're taking care of. I don't know what those other operations are, but I know they're way beyond my capabilities. Let it go now.

'Let me guess, they told you they never hurt anyone who didn't deserve it?'

Correct, but again, I said nothing. Instead, I looked away through the doors that led into the garden, towards where Grace had been buried.

'It's not for you, Kai.'

You wouldn't understand, Ethan. You've never been in my position. You won't even see your son. You have no idea what you're capable of doing when you're desperate. You have no idea how far you would go to ensure you don't get burned alive. Even if it means selling your soul to the Crains.

'It's fine, Ethan.'

He rose from the sofa.

'I'm afraid I can't help you, Kai. Not if you're working with them. I have too much at stake.'

'It's fine, Ethan. We all need to look out for our own.'

I watched him leave as my eyes pierced into him,

pushing him further away from me. It was too late to save myself from the Crains, but at least I could save him.

Today

'They never hurt anyone who didn't deserve it.' I lay here and think about how much of that is true, now that I've had a metal rod impaled into my back and through my chest. Did I deserve this?

I know this isn't the work of the Crains. I can still breathe and that's not how they work. They'd have made me die a slow and painful death, one which didn't have room for morphine or any other painkiller.

I wonder, who decides the level of pain and destruction that's inflicted onto someone? This hollowness inside me tells me it could be anyone. We're all judges. We all judge unconditionally and we make those judgements upon our version of the truth. We act on it in the name of justification and I guess, after everything I have done, it was enough for someone to justify why it was okay for them to impale this pole into me. Someone out there believes I deserve it. Someone out there wants me dead.

I don't want to do this again. The last panic attack was bad enough and my heart can't take the strain. I need to hold out for a few more hours.

I wonder, was Patrick deserving of the life he was living all these years? I don't understand. I don't understand the laws of judging. I don't understand justice, karma. I don't understand any of it. How was he okay? How was he happy?

I'd placed Skye and Bella in one of the best schools in the city. They were able to enjoy their lives being free to buy whatever they wanted. They were happy growing up, and healthy. And it was me who did that for them. *Me*, the one man in my entire family who stuck around and did right by two kids that weren't even his. To give them what they had and more, I'd sold into the Crain's way of life without knowing the extent of what I was getting into. There was no way out, but it was worth it for the happiness of the twins. I did it for them.

A cloud of darkness moves over me as I realise that I'd been eating nothing but the fruits of poison whilst walking up a paper mountain. I was too busy being playing king, growing my empire without realising I was nothing but a sheep. A sheep being herded into a cage by a dog.

The guilt of leaving Mum in the care home feels like the acid in my guts is eating away at my insides slowly. I guess we were comfortable with our situation. Comfortable living at the top of a mountain that was sinking fast. I needed her. I needed her discipline and I needed her light because where I was heading, it was only dark.

Sixteen years ago

'Uncle Kai, you don't work at the coffee shop anymore?' Bella laid on the sofa where Ethan had been sitting not too long before.

'No, B. I left there a while back to take on another role.'

'I went there today to see you but they said you didn't work there anymore. Why did you leave?'

I guess I'm comfortable earning a higher salary for doing less. I'm working for the Crains, you know, delivering killers to houses so they can dismantle human beings only to stick them inside a box to be buried. I get paid a lot. How else are we able to afford all those brands you have wrapped around you?

'I'm a driver now, B. Deliveries.' I looked at her as she played with the strands of her long, shiny hair whilst conjuring up the next question for me to answer.

'What's with the secrecy? Are you still at the bar or have you quit that job too?'

'There are no secrets, B.' I smiled, encouraging a smile to creep onto her face too but I knew she was disappointed.

'Yes, I'm still at the bar. Sorry, I didn't mention it.'

Sorry I didn't mention how I've become so sloth-like to my responsibilities. Sorry I've been overly focused on my newfound family so that I can cash in on the pink Queen of England to give you everything you want.

'There are no secrets.' Sorry, I'm lying to you.

'Promise? We're family, remember, Uncle Kai? You used to tell us that all the time – family is important, family is everything. Remember? No secrets.'

'I remember, Bella. I promise, no secrets.'

Guilt. It tasted like vomit. It tasted like my insides were crushed into a tiny cube, forcing all the liquids into my mouth, spreading across my tongue so I could taste the bitterness of it. So I could taste the guilt that resided within me before it slowly leaked from the sides of my mouth, allowing the foul scent to linger into the air, threatening to leak my secret.

I lied to Bella and she knew it. The secret had spilled somewhere amongst the silence that came after that moment of interrogation. She lay there on the sofa, thinking it through. My answers, my reaction. What do you know Bella? What do you know?

'You'd tell me if you were in trouble, right?

'Of course, B. If you were ten I'd get you ice cream to shut you up. Tell me, what does it take for me to get a beautiful, fourteen-year-old to stop interrogating me?' I stood up and sat beside her as she moved up from the sofa.

'I love you, Uncle Kai.' Her arms wrapped around me as that taste of guilt filled my mouth again.

'I love you too, B, despite you being as annoying as you are.' I held her closer, tighter.

'As annoying as *you* are.' She giggled and squeezed me back.

Patrick had raped at least eight girls during the space of six years since I'd known him. He was an animal and he deserved what was coming to him. I had no guilt in gaining his trust to betray him. I didn't have an option. I couldn't walk away from the Crains and put my life, and Skye and Bella's, at risk. Patrick didn't work for them. His life wasn't at risk. He had a choice, and he chose to rape innocent people for his own pleasure. He needed to die. It was my duty, as a guardian of two girls, it was my duty to protect them from people like him. And Patrick, I decided, deserved to be destroyed.

When you're forced on spending too much time with someone, the hate inside you grows like weeds. I never maintained that garden within me and I let those weeds take over, with thicker stems and roots digging deep into my soul. The only way to stop it was to kill it. Kill it from the roots so it could never come back.

It was time to push the people off the mountain I was climbing. It was time to fight. It was time to fight the battle and fight the war, forgetting about compassion along my journey, so I could watch them fall from the top.

CHAPTER **ELEVEN**

I was too afraid to get out and fight the real bullies

When the world bites me, I want to bite back. One bite at a time as my venom slowly seeps into the skin of my enemy, my friend, anyone.

Today

Ivanova comes into my space and closes the curtain. A man follows behind her with a stethoscope around his neck. A bit of a cliché but I guess he's a doctor. He looks at my notes and the screen on the computer beside me and I quickly close my eyes and pretend I'm sleeping. I wonder why he's wasting his time with me when we all know I'm dying. Do doctors even work this late into the night? I assume it's late but I don't know what time it is because that clock, it's still not working. But that doesn't deter me, I know that time is still going by. And I know I don't have much of it left.

'Increase the oxygen and…'

I can't make out what he's saying through the noise that's bursting into my mask.

'…laying upright… Antibiotics.'

Is he only stressing some of the words or is it me? I hate this mask.

'Sepsis… lung…'

I'm not a doctor. I know that rod hit my lung, they explained that when they began to drain the mucus from it. But I'm sure I just heard him say I have sepsis. I'm not sure. I lift my shutters a little to take a peek at what's going on. Ivanova moves to the machine beside me and reduces my oxygen levels. Thank you. That gushing noise has become more bearable. Maybe she's not so bad after all.

'He hasn't even had anyone come to visit.'

The noise becomes louder again and I'm convinced Ivanova knows I'm listening. I'm convinced she wanted me to hear her. I feel a cold sensation hit me and I assume she's topped up my painkillers before leaving my space with her clunky keys and heavy footsteps.

I have sepsis. I turn to the clock. Although it's not moving, I know my time is running out.

I guess it's become human nature, not to be human. I guess we're all stuck under a spell that's making us believe that there's only one winner. I know now that's not true. But it's too late. I lost my moral compass a long time ago. I was climbing that mountain formed on a foundation of quicksand and I'd begun to sink. And instead of climbing out the hard way, I took an easy chance for survival, holding on to the devil's hand that had placed me onto a slippery slope only to let me slide all the way down. All the way here in this bed.

Fifteen years ago

'You've been ordered to take on a hit, Kai. You must go with Tyler to assist.'

The look on his face and the deepness in Vin's voice told me it wasn't an option.

Toni and Vin had a spot to fill and I was ready to step up and work towards initiation – becoming a real member of the Family.

'Across the street, is a black 2003 Maserati Quattroporte. You will walk towards it and get in from the rear left. Tyler will take it from there.' He turned his head to stare at the back of the headrest in front of him. 'He doesn't speak so follow his instruction. You'll know what to do when the time comes.'

He continued to stare forward. My cue to leave. I climbed out of the Range Rover as he glared into the headrest before I threw him behind the thick, black metal of the car door.

What are you getting yourself into, Kai? What is this? What happened to being an errand boy? What happened to just getting information? You're a hitman now, are you? How are you going to do this? How are you going to kill a person? What are you doing, Kai?

Tyler was already inside. I'd never met him, except once during a pick-up. The sound of the engine roared, jumpstarting my heart as it thundered in vibration with the car.

We were driven to a large mansion-looking house just outside the city. Tyler never spoke nor did he instruct, but I knew. I knew my job was about to take a turn for the worst.

Despite travelling up the mountain, I knew I was going down and I knew I was about to do things that I could never take back.

I wondered if the torture and torment that Tyler put this man through was a scare tactic. A warning to keep away from the Crains. A message maybe. I didn't know his name, but a child was there crying out for his dad as Tyler cut off bits from the man's body while I held him down. Blood spilled out of him faster than a deadly virus as we decorated the room with blotches of red.

I'd seen that man before. The driver. He was Toni and Vin's driver before me. I wondered what it was he did, and I wondered what they could do to me as I held this man down, watching him fighting the pain as he held onto his pride, dignity and strength in front of his wife and son. I stared at him as he watched Tyler move on to his wife, not able to do anything as he lay there, pathetic, with his tongue and chunks of his body lying beside him. The shrilling sounds of her screams shattered my soul as she refused to keep it together. She pushed back from the chair she was tied onto, with her eyes open wide and glaring right into Tyler's as he moved closer towards her. He pierced her skin with the knife forming waterfalls of blood as tears scaled down her face. Her eyes were now glued onto her baby who watched in horror from the corner of the room. I couldn't let him see. I stepped between them. She looked up at me, right before Tyler sliced deep into her throat for the final kill. I watched as the light from her eyes faded into emptiness, and she watched the same in mine.

Fear stormed around my body and pumped my heart viciously as Tyler presented me with the knife, nodding towards the man who had just been made to watch his wife get murdered. He was going to be my first kill. I had to do it. I felt my eyes darken in my desperation to fit in. I felt no heartbeat in my chest, no tears to well behind my sockets. I felt the icy chill of death crawl towards me, tickling the hairs on the back of my neck, whispering to me, telling me to bring silence to this room and take away this man's last breath. I allowed my desperation to claw its way through my morals and bite its way into my soul as I gently inserted my knife into his throat. I dropped to my knees and I pulled his last breath from his lungs.

When he was still and the room was silent, I had realised what we'd done and the extent of the mess I'd gotten myself into. This man was beyond recognition. Mutilated in disbelief. And it was me who did it.

I had helped not only kill a man, but torture him and his family too. I had reached my arm out to him only to take away his light as I pulled him into the darkness. I had become the demon I once used to fear, and for that, this man's blood would be imprisoned in my mind. I needed to get out. I was tied up feeling claustrophobic with nothing around me except space. Empty space.

I stepped out of the car and heaved over the wall of my front garden until my guts were being spilled out across the grass. I felt as though I had tied a noose around my own neck in a game of hangman against the devil, and my first loss was somebody else's life. It wasn't long until the rematch and I knew I wasn't going to win because death cannot be undone. I was already dead.

I could see him. Blank stares whilst lying there like a doll on the ground in a position that made it obvious that he wasn't asleep. I looked behind me as the car stood silently outside my house, waiting for me. I needed to fix myself up. I needed to shower and go back to work, back to my bar job to commit to my role as Patrick's friend. As a loyal member of the Crain Family, it was my duty. Otherwise, I'd end up dead in a pool of my own blood, with Skye and Bella beside me. That message, I knew it was for me.

I wanted out but I was too involved. I had agreed to give my full loyalty to the Crains. I had agreed to sign my soul to them in exchange for money but no amount of money could clear my conscience for taking a life. My hands were already red with Grace's blood, but that was different. *I* had killed a man. *I* had killed his wife. *I* had made a baby an orphan. *Their* blood was on *my* hands and now this orphaned child would become the property of the Crain Family. A piece of property to be raised by the wives, sisters and daughters of those Crain men, and bought up to be nothing more than another recruit into the family.

The fire will spread amongst a new generation. We'll burn each other until the entire planet turns to nothing but ashes, leaving not even the smallest fragment of goodness behind.

I have the image of blood, guts and death each time I close my eyes. I smell their burnt bodies and I hear their screams. I have the weight of blame and fault upon me and I remember the faces of each soul as I recall each night when I sat to ensure each of those men had died a slow and painful death for the sins they committed against the Crains.

I had fought battles for somebody else. *I* fought. *Me*. Someone who was once unable to stand up for himself, someone who had his little sister fight against the bullies his entire life. *Me*. I was a man who found his strength for the sake of earning a few thousand pounds. For the sake of earning respect. For the sake of revenge. And now? Now I'm a murderer because I was too afraid to get out and fight the real bullies.

I was stuck. I was stuck and forced to stay committed to the kind of people I had despised. I had to agree with whatever was asked of me. It was one of their rules. No questions, no disputes, just get the job done. In, out, get paid, done. If you're not with them, you're against them. And if you're against them, your family goes first and you're made to watch. No official will stop them. It's all done undercover, massive payouts. If you refuse a job, then it's the end game. Who would dare refuse? No one. No one alive to tell the story.

CHAPTER **TWELVE**

I forgot about me

It recognises things before you do, but it cannot be trusted as a keeper of secrets. It's disloyal to its person as it changes with emotion, suffocating man with too much or too little. It's a skill given to mankind yet not all are mindful to observe it. That's what makes it so precious. We're drowning in the air and we don't even know it. It's a delicate thing, breathing.

Today

I guess, when you're too busy focusing on helping others, you forget about yourself. I forgot about me. I forgot about the person I was and the life I wanted to live. I forgot about all of that. I had sinned in more ways than I could imagine, in ways that could never be forgiven. And for what?

Skye and Bella haven't even come to see me yet. I've been here for, I don't know how many days, but it seems like a long time and I don't think I have much more of it left. Everything I've ever done has gone unacknowledged, taken for granted as though it was my duty to live for them. But I can't be angry. I know I fucked up. But no matter what I've done, I know I don't deserve this and I know they know this too. They will come. I have hope. I guess hope is what a man needs at a time like this, when he has nothing left.

The struggle to breathe is well known to me, more so when the sounds are coming from somebody else. I can hear Mr Martinez in the bed opposite and it sounds like he's having trouble. I wonder what's haunting him as he sleeps. I wonder what he's done. He's crying out for someone like he does every night and I wonder whether I do the same.

He's struggling to breathe. I recognise the sound well. I can even see what his face looks like right now even with the curtains closed, his eyes too. I've seen it all too much. The struggles of a man fighting for his life despite knowing that the battle was never his to win. Martinez is close to losing his fight but it doesn't seem like he's leaving nicely. And now I'm wondering if it's really the case when people say 'he died peacefully in his sleep.' Mr Martinez doesn't sound like he's at peace. He sounds like he's in pain, stressed, fighting.

By the time Ivanova comes in, he'll be dead. Or it could even be Irene who finds him tomorrow. That's a long time. A long time for a man to lay there dead and opposite me. I wonder if this is the karma that I'm having to face for all those lives I've taken and walked away from. Now I must sleep with a dead man laying opposite me. Although I know he's still breathing, I also know it won't be for long.

I need Ivanova to take him away. Despite what I've done, there's something about dead bodies that brings fear upon me. The fear of how peaceful they look when they've departed. How their face and shoulders fall as they relax into their final resting place. I fear the feeling that passes into me. To see how the victory is theirs because they no longer have to fight this war. Sometimes I want to be there, away from the fight. But here I am, still fighting. Still fighting when I could be sleeping like the rest of the souls that are no longer trapped.

The Crains would dispose of the bodies within minutes of removing the soul from them. They had people do that for them. Other associates hired specifically for that job, the job of clearing up the mess. Soon, Mr Martinez will become that mess, and the nurses will tell his family that he died peacefully in his sleep. I know better.

I wonder who he cries out for, whether he has a family. He hasn't had any visitors since I've been here, but then, neither have I. And with that thought, I can feel my chest begin to tighten up.

Ivanova comes running into my space with three other nurses who I assume only visit me when I'm asleep because I've never seen them before. I'm trying to point to Martinez's cubicle but they aren't paying attention. They're playing around with my oxygen levels while Martinez is dying opposite me. He needs saving but they're all here with me and I wonder what's going on. It pains me to keep my arm up but I do. I keep my fingers pointed towards the direction of Martinez in the hope that one of these four nurses here with me can read the sign, but they don't. I don't know this man, yet I want to save him. A sudden thought runs through me as I realise this is an act of selfishness. My attempt to save this dying stranger wouldn't free me from the sins that I have already committed. I lower my arm as the morphine that's just been injected into it surges inside me. I try to relax but I can still hear him suffocating and I don't understand why the nurses aren't listening. His breathing is slowing and I can tell that he's not far off from becoming a 'mess'. But Ivanova is here with three other nurses, taking care of *me*. I'm confused and I don't understand why they're all crowding around me. For a second I think I may be hallucinating, or even worse, dead. Ivanova comes close. She takes off my mask and I realise it's me. I'm the one who's struggling to breathe.

Fifteen years ago

'You good?' The sound of Toni's whisper had scraped through my eardrums, sharper than the tools I used to commit my sin. The sound of his voice was that of a raging fire, whilst the smile that was spread across his face, a pitchfork. The devil had come to applaud.

Do you expect me to be feeling good? I've just aided in torturing a man and his wife before taking their lives in front of their child. How was I going to be feeling good, Toni?

My insides became heavy as it dawned on me, the person I was becoming. I was no far off from those people you see in films or on the news, those who commit crimes and go back to their daily routine as if nothing had happened. Just over an hour before, I had been murdering a man and his wife in front of their baby, now there I was, serving alcohol to overly paid businessmen who needed a drink because *they* had a hard day at work. I was becoming the type of person that the papers and the public would brand a psychopath. A twisted and cold-hearted psychopath. But that wasn't true. I had remorse, I knew right from wrong. I was, plain and simply put, a cold-hearted murderer.

'I'm good.' I poured him a glass of whisky without ice, knowing he preferred it with.

'I'm not staying. Best you drink it, you look like you need it.' Toni pushed it back to me whilst leaning into the bar towards me, nodding for me to come close. I moved forward towards my master.

'You know, we are all human. We are the most dangerous of all the animals on earth. We take more lives than the black mamba, than the smallest mosquito, we are greater than the great shark and wilder than the hungriest lion. Did you know that a lion hunts when he is hungry? We human's, we hunt even when our pantry is fully stocked. We kill, not to eat but to shed blood and watch it spill. So we can paint the town red. That's how we mark our territory. That's how we claim our own. We take it, and we leave behind a big red mark. We're a different type of animal, us humans, the type that no one can mess with. I hope that you can understand my point here, my friend.'

He looked up at me and I nodded, accepting his threat before he moved away.

'Good job today.' He walked out. I had realised then that I'd signed not only my life away to the Crain Family, but Skye and Bella's too.

'Kai!' Patrick had been seated away from the bar. It was his usual Friday drinks with his R.E.L colleagues.

'The usual, mate, and a bottle of white for the newbies.' He placed his card on the bar. 'Make it two, they aren't in a rush to get home tonight.'

He winked at me as I peeled the card from the sticky slab of wood and keyed his order into the machine. He leaned further into the bar. It had become a regular occurrence for people who wanted to speak to me in private whilst being in public.

'What was that about, Kai? You're not still working with them are you?' The look on his face told me he was concerned as he turned his thumb to the door, pointing in the direction that Toni had left in. I was surprised he gave a shit.

'Kai?' Patrick waved his hand in my face.

Yes, Patrick. I am working with them. I am working with them and just before I came here, I scrubbed away another man's blood from my body. And do you want to know what I did before that? I killed him. Just after mutilating him and witnessing the sharpness of cold steel strike across his wife's neck. I did all of that, and now I'm here, standing behind the bar, serving overly paid assholes like you who waste their salary on drowning their sorrows caused by having real jobs they hate. You want to know why Patrick? Because we're all stuck in this game called life that society has put us in, and the only way to escape it, is death.

'Kai?'

'What? No, of course not. He was paying off a tab from earlier, that's all. Who are those chicks you're with?' I nodded to the corner where Patrick had been sitting.

'The new assistants they bought in to support everyone who'd been promoted to director. You see that hot one over there, the brunette with the glasses?'

I knew bringing up the girls would throw him off. He never could sniff around in my business for long, no matter how large his nose was.

We both looked towards a tall and slim, teen-aged-looking girl with thick black frames and bright red lipstick. She looked like a sophisticated hooker in the making.

'She's my PA, here to assist me in all my personal, you know…' He winked at me as though I would approve.

I placed two bottles of wine and a pint of beer on the bar and gave him back his card.

'It's on the house. Have a good night.' I moved

aside to wave over the next customer in line. I was in no mood to talk, especially to a condescending rapist who was about to tell me who his next victim was going to be. I glanced over to his PA, making a mental note of her face as a prompt to put in an anonymous call to the police the moment they left my sight.

'Pretty busy tonight! Sorry, mate. Will catch you later.' I yelled over to him as he walked back to his colleagues. I still had a job to do for the Crains and I wasn't willing to mess that up, especially not after the threat I'd just received from Toni.

Today

'Happy birthday, Mr Jackson, I'm glad to see you today!'

Irene walks into my space, waking me up from my thoughts. The sun is out, I can tell because I'm struggling to open my eyes. It's a lot brighter than what I'm used to and I can only assume that the curtains between myself and Mr Kahele are open.

My assumption proves to be true as my eyes adjust to the extra light. I see open space and I feel exposed. I don't like it.

'I hear we nearly lost you last night.'

I forgot about last night. It feels like a long time ago now but the mention of it brings it back to me in small bits and I feel like I'm suffering from a case of short term memory loss.

Irene smiles at me as she tops me up with water and morphine before walking around to check if my bag needs emptying. It doesn't. She scribbles in the files at the end of my bed.

'I'll be back soon okay, Mr Jackson? Get you all cleaned up for your big day.'

She's smiling at me again and I can see it's genuine. She's a nice nurse. She makes me feel a lot more relaxed than Ivanova, who I'm no longer sure still wants to kill me. I remember her being here last night. She saved my life and now I'm confused and wondering if I've been paranoid this entire time.

Irene turns towards Mr Kahele.

'We'll need to leave these open again, just to be on the safe side.' She leaves me exposed to the rest of the unit.

I have more space around me with these curtains open but I somehow feel like a prisoner. The walls of my cell need sanding down and a fresh lick of paint and someone needs to light a fragrance candle or something because all I can smell is vegetable soup. Pre-made, packaged soups lingering through the corridors yet there is no one in my room well enough to eat.

I'm wondering why they saved me last night when all that's left for me to do is die. It doesn't make sense and I can't help but think that maybe the Crains have paid the nurses to keep me alive only to torture me later. I don't know if this kind of treatment is normal. Do they really do this much for someone who is going to die? They've already told me that they can't do anything to help me, so why do they care so much? It doesn't make sense. I assure myself they're not getting paid by the Crains because even they don't have that kind of power. But they're doing so, so much to help me be comfortable and I don't understand.

I wonder what happened last night. Irene said they'd nearly lost me but I don't remember clearly. My face feels sore and I lift my arm a little to move my mask. It's as tight as the hold that the Crains had over me and I'm suffocating just the same. I stop as a sudden pain shoots into my chest, the same pain I felt last night and I remember pointing towards Martinez's bed. Now I'm pretty sure it was Martinez who was having trouble breathing and not me. Why is Irene lying to me? She wouldn't. She's the nice one. I decide I may have been hallucinating, imagining Martinez dying when maybe it was me after all.

'Give me five minutes, Mr Jackson.' Irene walks across the room from Mr Kahele's space, pushing her trolley along with her as the contents of the metal draws scrape against them. I don't feel comfortable by that sound as it takes me back. Back to the moment when I crawled onto the road with this rod scraping against the concrete.

I remember a car. It was dark but I remember now, that a car was there, I remember it stopping to... save me? I need to do this. I need to remember.

My oxygen mask is large enough to cover my nose and mouth and it's fixed firmly on my face. The suction is stronger than before and it hurts. I can hear bouts of air passing through the tubes and into my nose and mouth. It's uncomfortable but I assume they've increased my oxygen levels to help me breathe better. But it doesn't. It only makes me feel as though I've been thrown out of a plane, and without a parachute.

I wonder whether Martinez has one on too. I glance over to his bed, but it's empty.

CHAPTER **THIRTEEN**

My inner voice, it speaks the truth, but only to me

How much does one have to suffer before he turns to worship Satan himself? I wonder. I wonder why we must be so hostile to one another. They say much of the cruelty in the world is driven by insecurities. They say even the compassionate of people can turn. I guess it's true, that maybe kindness is the deadliest form of weakness in mankind. You get left behind for being kind. Maybe it's an insecurity, being too kind, trying to please others. Maybe life isn't supposed to be about other people. Maybe it's supposed to be about ourselves.

Two years ago

'Uncle Kai, what did Mum do before she died?'

Skye and Bella laid on separate ends of the sofa, Bella glaring out into the garden under the apple tree where Grace had been buried, and Skye reading Michel Foucault's *Madness and Civilisation* for the third time. I sat on the single sofa beside them, sipping on my tea as though I hadn't just killed another man, acting like it was any normal Sunday afternoon at home with the girls.

'Work-wise, what did she do?'

Your mum had you when she was fifteen, she dropped out of school, decided not to involve the guy who knocked her up, and she dedicated the rest of her life staying home doing everything she could for you two, before she gave up and killed herself, of course. Before she left all of that responsibility on me.

Maybe it's a good thing that I don't use my inner voice on the outside. It speaks to me differently from my outer voice. It tells me things that no one needs to hear. My inner voice, it speaks the truth but only to me.

'She was studying to be a nurse.' I lied. I don't know whether it was to protect them, or Grace.

'What about Grandma?' Skye peeked her eyes over the top of the book. The twins had always been curious but it had taken them at least twenty years to sit down and ask me.

'Grandma cleaned houses and supplied

homemade jam to a local bakery store when the neighbour's strawberry plant grew over into our garden.'

That was true. Although she'd given up work after I'd come back from university without consulting me because she assumed that I alone would be fine to work three jobs to feed five people as well as take on the responsibility of taking care of the rest of the household finances.

'Is that why you love jam so much?' Bella wriggled around on the sofa.

'I guess so.'

'Thanks for taking care of us, Uncle Kai. Happy birthday.' Skye picked up a box from behind the cushion.

'Happy birthday, Uncle Kai.' Bella followed, picking up another as they both stood up.

I knew what it was - a jar of homemade jam just like every year. Strawberry jam from Skye, and marmalade from Bella. I guess, despite having so many riches, the gift of homemade jam was the real luxury. The scent of childhood, the warmth of happiness, the taste of life.

Yet that year, it wasn't the jam that made my birthday so special, it was gratitude. The gratitude from Skye and Bella who, for the first time, decided to tell me I was appreciated on my forty-sixth birthday. I had finally proven I was worthy of love.

After years of being nobody, I became somebody. Although, Mum and Grace were no longer around to see.

Today

I know they'll come today. I know they'll come so I can smell the scent of homemade jam again. I wonder whether Mum felt how I do right now, as I have been for the past few days as I wait for Skye and Bella to come and visit, holding on to that last bit of hope I have left before I float away. I wonder how long Mum held onto hope for. I see now, that no amount of love from a carer or a nurse can add up to the love felt from a single visit by someone you love. I let her down.

She died in that home, surrounded by strangers. I don't know if it made her feel uneasy, I don't know if she was already dying. I guess, if I had visited or even called I would have known. Either way, I am grateful. I'm grateful that she didn't suffer. I'm grateful that from all of the ways she could have left, she chose to die in the middle of the night, peacefully in her sleep.

A burning sensation is starting to run through me as I look over at Mr Martinez's empty bed. All the thoughts and disturbances in my head over the past few days have made me see that no matter what I was told, I know that Mum didn't die peacefully. And that was because of me.

I look around me, desperately trying to get to know some of these men in my room. Mr Kahele is asleep, as is the guy in front of him. I don't know his name, but he's been in a coma since I've been here and the nurses don't speak to him. As for Martinez, he's dead. I don't know anything about these people and they don't know anything about me. But I do know something. I do know that we are a bunch of bodies who are refusing to die because we still have the need to fulfil the requirements of our unfinished business. I don't know what theirs are, but mine is to find out who put me in here.

'Sorry, Mr Jackson.'

Irene has come back into my space after a longer time than she had said. She's closing the curtains and I guess she's preparing to bathe me. I don't see the point of this, especially when I'll be leaving soon, like Mr Martinez. I wonder what happened to him.

Irene glides the sponge down my arm. It's warm and it feels soothing. I move my arm towards my face to remove the mask. I want to talk to her but her gentle touch moves my arm away.

'You need to keep this on, Mr Jackson.'

I point to Martinez's empty bed.

'I'm sorry, Mr Jackson. Mr Martinez had some complications last night.' Irene stops bathing me and looks at me apologetically.

I wonder whether those complications were because the nurses were all in here with me. I hope that's not another death on my hands. I don't know how much of this I can take anymore, especially now that I'm about to face my creator, which I believe could be the devil.

'We can say a prayer for your friend if you wish.' She moves to my legs. What do you mean by 'my friend,' Irene? I don't understand. I'm confused. I reach for my mask as my chest crumbles inside me but the earlier dose of morphine seems to be doing something. The volcano hasn't erupted just yet.

'You both came in together. You don't remember?' Irene is looking at me as she dips the sponge in water. I shake my head a little. Fuck, this is painful.

'You were crouched over in the back of his car, Mr Jackson.'

My head is feeling a little funny. I came in with Martinez? Who was he? He wasn't one of the Crains, was he? I don't remember working with him. Why would I be in a stranger's car? I don't get it. I was hiding in a garage, I remember that, but there were no cars around, not that I can recall. How did I know Martinez?

I feel light-headed and I'm trying to think back to the day I got impaled by that dirty, rusty rod. Something doesn't feel right. I can see red. I see the pavement and I can taste the blood that's spilling from my mouth and I think I'm about to die on the side of the road. The driver. Someone tried to save me. Mr Martinez, he tried to save me. What is happening? How did I forget this? It was Martinez's car. He bought me to this hospital. He was driving. Fast. We were being followed, I think we were anyway. Oh my God, oh God. I feel sick. I need to be sick. My mouth is filling up with saliva and— Irene, Irene please pay attention—I need to be sick. I can feel my blood racing around my body. I can feel it being pumped around faster than a bullet to my brain. My heart is working overtime and I don't know if I'm about to have another tremor or a heart attack. Or die. I can feel something seize up in my chest and it feels like I've been struck with another metal shaft. I can hear my machine beeping and Irene has left me. I don't know where she's gone. God, I can't believe it. The gunshots. They shot him, more than once. I remember. I remember now. Whoever wanted me dead took a shot at Martinez. They shot him.

My heart sinks as the volcano inside me begins to erupt, spilling hot lava into the room. I have to do this, I'm close, I can feel it. Think, Kai. Think.

Gunshots. Who? Did they impale a rod through me despite having a gun? Who was it, Kai? Who was it? I'm back to thinking it was the Crains again, and maybe inserting that rod was just the beginning of my torture. If they wanted me dead straight away they'd have used the gun on me too, but they wanted to torture me. My heart is racing and I'm worried about the safety of Skye and Bella.

'Okay, Mr Jackson, stay with us, you can't keep doing this.'

Irene comes back with two other nurses. They each take their roles. While Irene messes with my mask, another is injecting liquids of some sort into the bags hanging above me, and the other says she is trying to stabilise my breathing. She plays with the oxygen levels and I can feel my mask get tighter as the sound of oxygen spilling from the tubes gets louder. They're moving fast, panicking, and I'm panicking too. I feel like I'm having a seizure but I need to survive. I need to. I need to find out what is happening, I need to protect them. The twins, they're in danger. They're counting on me.

'Come on, Mr Jackson, you can do this.'

Yes, Kai, come on.

CHAPTER **FOURTEEN**

Family is everything

With a fluorescent charm that shines against the ambers of the sunlight, warmth creeps into the air. It glistens brighter than a sunrise over a still ocean and it blinds all that it touches as it glides across the earth, claiming what doesn't belong.

Today

From the first time I saw you girls smile, I knew what I wanted in life. Happiness. I wanted all the happiness in the world so that I could give it all to you. I promised your mum, before that last layer of dirt was sprinkled over her grave, that I would do whatever it took to make sure those smiles never left. I promised her I'd always protect you, that you'd come before anything else. I may have failed you, and for that, I am sorry.

Rossi Crain was the King of the Crain Family. He was a man that many had respected, out of fear and out of love. He saved as many as he would harm and he believed his soul was cleaner than the disinfected surfaces on which bodies would lie. He himself had never spilled the blood of another man with his own hands, despite paying for the chemicals that were used to hide away the acts of murder. The acts of murder that were demanded by the sounds that came from his mouth. Rossi Crain was the man who would decide another man's fate, the man who would decide the level of pain another man deserves.

I sometimes wondered whether he was real. He was often spoken of but never seen, especially by those like me. I didn't know where he lived or how he made the decisions he made. I wondered whether they were as tough as they seemed to be. Rossi, Toni, Vin. But then I'd hear the screams, I'd see the blood and I'd see the fight disappear in the eyes of all of the men I killed and helped to kill in the name of the Crains and it would bring everything back to life. Rossi Crain was the devil himself, and I worked for him.

Thirteen years ago

'I tried to call you, Uncle Kai. Your friends are here to see you but your phone was going to voicemail.'

A chill ran through me as I entered the living room. They're not my friends, Skye. Not at all.

'I hope you don't mind us popping in, Kai.' Toni glared at me as he took his last sip of water from his cup and I wondered how long they'd been in my home.

'Of course not. Make yourself at home.' Make yourself at home like you already have, snooping around my living room, sitting with my nieces. A short moment of silence wrapped around me as Toni's eyes pierced through me, waiting for the realisation of what was happening to be slapped across my face. How did they know where I lived?

'Your mum was a fine-looking young woman, I see where you both get your beauty from.' He picked up a photo of Grace from the shelf that sat over the fireplace. 'It's such a sad way to die, but I can see that your Uncle is taking care of you extremely well.'

Toni looked over to me. There was something about his smile, something strange in his voice and just like that, I felt like the enemy.

'Grace would be proud of you, Kai.'

How did he know all of this? This whole time I had fooled myself about having mutual respect and keeping family and business separate, it was all bullshit. I should have known better. Of course, they would check me out. Of course, they'd need to know my entire history. This was the Crain Family I was working for. Hell, even the Queen of England wouldn't have done this much of a detailed background check on me even if I worked at Buckingham Palace. I could see it, this was a threat, this was a warning, a notice from the Crains to remind me who I was working for and the consequences of what could happen if I were to fuck up now. What did I do wrong?

'You know, girls, your Uncle was telling me you're both at Ravenford College? My son studies History there. Gabriel.'

I stood there, grounded to the floor of the living room, watching as this lorry came in at full speed, striking me and knocking my soul from my body, crushing my insides like a can made from aluminium.

What do you want to do with the girls, Toni? I felt myself crumble a little. I needed to save them but I was frozen. I imagined myself building a brick wall around my innocent young girls, to keep them safe, to make sure the big bad wolves couldn't get in, but my bricks were made of Lego. Plastic pieces of building blocks that melted under the pressures of a fire's heat. Leave them out of this, Toni. Their souls are not yours.

'Oh, I know G. There's only one Gabriel in History.' Skye blushed a little. There was more to this conversation than it seemed.

I remained numb to the room and everything within it as I stared at Toni, proud and joyful as if playing a game.

I don't know much about you, Toni, yet you seem to know a lot about me and the girls. Tell me, was this a part of your plan all along? What is your business with these girls? Who is this Gabriel you say is your son? Is he also an employee of the Crains? It doesn't make sense, Toni. Of all the colleges in the area, it can't have been a coincidence that your 'son' goes to the same one as the twins, and also happens to study the same course as Skye. What game are you playing here, Toni? Why do I not know the rules?

'Can I get you another drink?' There I was, sitting in their hands like a Tamagotchi while they pushed all the buttons to control my every move.

I had killed at least six men and two women and had made three children orphans. I had befriended and bailed out a man who had raped over nine different women on various occasions, all for the sake of holding on to my loyalty to the Crains. And here they were, sitting in my home, reminding me not to cross the line. But that wasn't the worst of it.

A few weeks later, Toni and Gabriel had arrived for dinner unannounced – an act that became a regular occurrence.

'We're practically family now.' Toni and Gabriel had made their way to the dining table with a dish of spaghetti and clams.

'Family means everything to us Italians you know. It's a part of our culture. Family is very important, isn't it, Kai?' Toni was getting comfortable as he sat and preached over dinner. 'As men, it is our duty to do right by them.'

'Of course, family is everything,' I said, feeling the wrath of betraying Mum. I wondered whether Toni disrespected me for what I did to her. He never bought it up but his glare was enough to tell me that he knew. Of course, he knew.

'Thank you for the magnificent cuisine.' He hadn't touched our Chinese takeaway and had eaten only the spaghetti and clams that he bought with him.

'You're welcome.' Skye smiled as she excused herself to clear the table.

'Wait. Wait. I have something for us all.' The calmness in Toni's voice made the waves of the ocean roll into the room but the deepness and sharpness in his eyes was firm and authoritative, a reminder that a tsunami could hit at any moment.

'You put coffee in it.' He handed a small wooden bowl-like ornament to Bella. 'It's an old tradition in Italy, to sip from this cup after dinner.'

The cup was a smooth, handcrafted piece of wood with five spouts protruding from it.

'A coupe de l'amitie is what it's called. Or a friendship cup. You add coffee to it and share it amongst friends after dinner. Make some coffee, I'll show you.'

And with that, I watched as my niece scampered to the kitchen to follow an order from Toni.

'In Italy, we have these. Everyone at the dinner table must take a sip from this cup. It's passed around until everyone has taken a sip, but you mustn't put the friendship cup down until the round is completed.'

I guess, despite his words about being family, this friendship cup signified that we were not. We weren't family. We weren't even friends. I knew it and he knew it, yet we both continued to pretend that we were. His reason, for the sake of business, mine, to protect the life of Skye, who was dating his 'son', and Bella, who was soon to become his bitch.

Toni had taken the first sip of coffee through the cup as part of his 'Italian' tradition. He passed it to me and I took a sip before passing it on to Skye. She smiled, finding the whole thing awkward as she took a sip and passed it to Gabriel.

'Oh, it's strong!' Gabriel had put the wooden cup onto the table.

'G, I thought you can't put…' Skye had spoken only to be interrupted by Toni.

'I hope you aren't superstitious. Because it's believed that placing the cup down before it has been passed around, brings bad luck.' He smirked.

Bella's coffees were weaker than a house of straw in a cyclone. There was no way Gabriel would have considered it to be too strong. Toni, that conniving little prick had the whole charade planned out.

I wondered if this was the beginning of my torture. But it didn't make sense. I hadn't made a move. I hadn't spilt any secrets to Patrick, I had no intention to mess up their plan. Patrick and I had been friends for a long enough time for him to trust me. I was ahead of the game. I'd given them all the information they needed and more.

Today

My brain is working overtime right now and it seems like this new bout of oxygen is helping me think clearer. I gave them dirt on Patrick and R.E.L in order for them to know and understand everything about him. Which has only got me thinking, who was befriending me to get all the intel on me? Was Patrick working for the Crains too? But I've never told him about Skye or Bella, even Mum and Gracie. Could Mum have told someone in her care home? Did it go that far back that the Crains had someone working there? Wait, wait. Is that why Mum died? Did they kill her like they killed Martinez? Could it be the twins? I'm getting paranoid. I'm close. I can feel it. Someone in my circle is untrustworthy but who? How would Toni know about my past?

Gabriel. Of course. Skye would have told Gabriel. God, Skye, didn't I always teach you to keep our family business private? I guess that was easy, but that still doesn't tell me who wants me dead. I ignore the question that's lingering in the back of my mind. How did Gabriel know what course to study and which college to go to in the first place?

The Crains were smart. Toni and Vin possessed immense intelligence and knowledge. I realise now that they were playing me like I had been playing Patrick. While I was fake befriending Patrick, they were fake befriending me. But what did they need from Skye? How did they know I was going to fuck up? Unless... Did they already know before? Did they know then, what I know now? Fuck. Was this always a part of their plan?

Three months ago

'Bella, what's wrong?'

'I know I have you and everything, but I'm thirty now. Skye has G and they're always together. They're practically married now, Uncle Kai. Thirteen years is a long time to be with someone, and here's me hanging with you.'

Thirteen years? Is that how long it's been? A part of me wished that despite how this began, that Gabriel's love for Skye was real. Otherwise, thirteen years is a long time to fake a relationship for the sake of business.

'Uncle Kai?'

'Sorry, B. I'm listening. What's wrong with hanging around with me?'

I threw a cushion at her but it was too late. She'd made her way into the garden to sit with Grace.

Today

I can feel pain in my abdomen, and I can feel my gut clenching as it hits me that I've continued my false friendship with Patrick for a lot longer than thirteen years for the sake of business. For the sake of not getting killed, for the sake of my nieces. It wasn't about money. That dream died a long time ago. It was about survival, and no amount of pinks could buy that.

I look back at how it all started. Over a stupid few words that Patrick had said in front of his friends and just like that, Toni and Vin walk in and there I was, standing there like a punching bag falling for every hit. I was working, earning better money than Patrick. I'd get paid in pinks and I worked for a family more powerful than that of the Queen of England. I worked for the King, and he'd shower me with fifties. This is what I'd always wished for, and boy, did I hate it.

And just like that, Toni and Vin walk in. Was it really 'just like that' all those years ago? Right place, right time, as though they had walked in on cue? Did Patrick set me up, only for me to set him up? What is happening? Was that a part of their act? To catch me on a bad day so that I could stick my hand out to Toni and Vin's proposal and sign my life away?

It doesn't make any sense. I still can't think of this as being the work of the Crains, me lying here. I've seen how far they can go. I've seen what they're capable of doing. Yet I can't help but feel that maybe they were involved in some way or another, because no one has come to see me yet. Not Toni, not Vin, Gabriel or even Skye and Bella.

Someone's just walked into my space and I really don't want to open my eyes but I can smell something. Could it be? I'm afraid it's a hallucination. I can smell something sweet, like home, with Mum and Gracie. My heart feels fluttery as something tells me that they're here, that they've come, Skye and Bella! But I'm afraid to open my eyes. I have so many questions and this may be my only chance to find out what happened, and the last time I see them again. But I'm scared.

I'm scared of how I'll react when I see them, how they'll react when they see me. But I'm so happy they've come. I feel nervous and I don't understand why. It's only been a few days, or at least I think it has. I can't believe they're going to see me like this. I hope it doesn't destroy them. I still see Grace lying on the floor when I try to sleep at night and I don't want the same for them. Maybe I should pretend to be sleeping. Maybe by waking up I'll do more damage than good. But I've been waiting for so long. I've been dying to see them. Maybe we can talk a little, and we can figure this out. Maybe they have information. My mind is racing. They're here. They're safe.

I open my eyes slowly letting the light trickle in. There's a figure sitting beside me. My eyes are a little blurred, but not enough to blind me. I can see that the twins are not here and I can't help but feel like I'm walking down a dark mountain of disappointment as it swallows me up, burying me within the emptiness of hope, deeper than six feet. I begin to acknowledge how unfortunate my level of judgement has always been. I would be a fool to think that the girls will come.

The man who attempted to kill me might be here and I don't think I want to know who it is anymore. I don't think I care. I feel empty inside. Do it, I'm here. Kill me already.

'Don't mind me, I hope you don't mind a bit of company on your birthday.'

Irene's voice echoes through my ears and I'm disappointed that my fight isn't over.

I used to believe that death was the loss of life, of those you love, those you care about. I was afraid of losing someone because of the feelings I felt when I'd lost my sister. But I know now that if there's anything to be afraid of, it's the loss of what's within you when you're still alive. That hope.

I look over to Irene as she sits beside me. She's reading the paper whilst eating a sandwich and I'm sure, I'm sure I know this smell. The scent of jam masks her cigarette smell well. I know it's fresh, I know it's homemade. It reminds me of Mum and Grace and, wow, I feel peaceful.

Irene rustles her newspaper and I get another

whiff of her sandwich. It takes me away to the happy moments and I feel calm. But there is something that's creeping around inside me and I'm wondering, what made Irene choose to eat a jam sandwich for lunch today of all days?

Is someone teasing me? Is this subtle torture? It's too subtle for it to be the Crains. Maybe the twins are sending me a sign that they're safe? Or maybe they aren't. Irene hasn't told me anything. She's halfway through her sandwich and she hasn't mentioned them or strawberry jam. I feel as though I'm a piece of meat being hung from a hook, dangling over an open cage waiting for the lions to be let out of their dens to feast on my flesh, and that too in front of an audience.

I can't believe that this scent, this scent that once bought me happiness, I can't believe it has transformed into something that keeps me under a blanket of blackness.

I realise now that happiness is no more than a vivid dream. Darkness has taken over, turning my dreams into nothing but shadows as they become lost like the souls that live among it. It doesn't come in riding a wave in the distance, it lurks beneath me. It hits me from the bottom, pulling me down by my feet, paralyzing me from the bottom up making sure I can still see, making sure I can still smell. Strawberry jam. Why?

CHAPTER **FIFTEEN**

Who really cares anymore?

I embrace the darkness, even on the most moonlit of nights. I find the shadows and avoid the pools of light. Give it time, and you'll realise you're better off in the darkness. For in the darkness, your senses will be heightened and you won't be blinded.

We were always meant to live in darkness, even with the light. Five billion years from now the sun will stop shining and darkness will win. It's supposed to win. It's inevitable. Darkness will come and the world will become a cold and sinister place to live in, if it isn't already.

They couldn't pick on me for wearing secondhand clothes anymore, they couldn't pick on me for having the same lunch every day anymore, and they couldn't pick on me for having my little sister as my voice anymore. But they'd still find something else to say, something else to whisper about. Even with over one hundred thousand pounds sitting in my account, and more in cash stashed away in different parts of the house, I was still that kid. The barman. The paperboy. The man whose sister killed herself. The man who put his mum in a home. The one who was left to raise his nieces alone. I was still a nobody.

Two months ago

'Chasing money is a fine art. Like a game of chess. One bad move and it's over.'

Unlucky for me then. I don't know how to play chess, Patrick.

I didn't tell him. I wasn't going to give him another bit of ammunition to fire back at me in front of his friends. Who has time for chess?

I stared at him, sitting across the table from me in the dinginess of the bar as he spoke to me about what once was my favourite subject.

'I could have been stuck behind this bar like you, you know.' He slammed his pint down on the table after taking his first sip of the night.

But you're not, because you weren't desperate. You didn't have to settle for the first job that came up. You didn't have anybody relying on you. You didn't have the weight of the world on your shoulders. That was me. I did.

My inner voice screamed at him, but my outer voice remained silent, letting him belittle me, letting him make me feel like working in a bar made me inadequate to what he was.

'But you've got to be smart to be where I am. You need to make sure you're in so you can speak to the right people. That's what networking is about. It doesn't matter what you know, you just have to have something they want. Subtle bribery. It's a thing that goes on within all businesses. You've heard of it, right? They prefer to call it "networking," but it's more of a "you scratch my back and I'll scratch yours," kind of thing.'

I leaned in closer to the table, taking a mental note of every word. Maybe he's about to give me some inside information about R.E.L that the Crains don't even know about. I wondered what that could be worth. I nodded my head, encouraging him to carry on.

'Networking is just a bunch of people together in the same room and they all want to give you something in return for something back. And most of the time it's not even money. You find out what they want and find someone who can give it to them. No one ever does something for nothing, not in business, not even in life.'

He wasn't wrong. I'd befriended him for money way before the Crains came into the picture, way back when he'd told me to keep the change, when I saw his clothes, when I found out he worked for R.E.L. Damn, I didn't realise I would stoop so low as to let it turn into some kind of friendship. Betrayal from the start. We weren't even friends.

His game to get rich was through moving up with R.E.L, and mine through moving up with the Crains. If you consider success to be luxuries and a lot of money, then we were both very much successful. Both our roles carried some form of respect in their own way, but to get there we'd both fucked over so many people.

'You're never happy with what you have. You always want more, and the more you have the blinder you become. That's the reality of it. And these people at R.E.L, they were blinder than the three blind mice. Myself included.'

He sipped his beer as he watched me glare at him.

Little do you know you are blinded by our "friendship". Little do you know I am also playing a part in this networking game. I need a decent salary, the Crains need you. Oh, you can't hear me, can you, Patrick? My inner voice, it's the keeper of all my secrets. I wonder, what do you need from me,

Patrick? What is your inner voice hiding from me?

'I'm out. Got a long shift tomorrow.' I wasn't liking where my train of thought was taking me. I was sitting with a rapist, comparing the differences between us. Me and my biggest enemy, we had more similarities than anything else. I wondered if that was why I hated him so much. Because I hated me too. I tried to think which one of us was worse but I wouldn't let myself admit it. I guess his game plan was smarter, more acceptable than mine because he wore a suit and worked in an office.

'You know, Kai, It's a circle. Everything and everyone. Somehow, we're all connected. We're all connected in one way or another, maybe it goes way back to our past, back to our ancestors even. Maybe you know someone I know, or you know someone who knows someone I know. As big as it seems, this world is small. Networking only brings those connections together. We're all linked and we all have use for one another, be it a lesson to learn or a lesson to teach.'

He sounded familiar, like Toni maybe. I stared at him, a little threatened by his ability to portray such a conclusion onto me with that high level of confidence. I was also taken aback at the level of intelligence that projected from him. This was Patrick, surely, the real Patrick before the alcohol took over.

'Sorry, mate. Got a bit deep there didn't I? It's bullshit anyway. This whole connection thing. It's something someone told me a long time ago. It was bullshit then too. Clearly need to drink.'

He laughed at himself and almost instantly with the flick of a switch, something changed in his eyes and he began to laugh at me.

'For a second there, I thought you were interested in all of that shit, Kai. Get a drink, won't you? Let's have a real conversation. None of this girly shit. Go, grab a pint.'

I wanted to go home but I got up and dragged my legs across the bar to grab myself another drink.

Today

I hear the rustling of paper and I open my eyes. Irene has finally finished her sandwich and is shaking crumbs off the newspaper. Her reading glasses are hanging from a lanyard around her neck and I'm wondering whether she's been pretending to read this entire time. I assume she's here out of sympathy but if that's the case, then the shaking of the paper is intentional and I can also assume she's only trying to wake me. I wonder why she wants me to be awake. I wonder if she knows something, maybe Skye and Bella are coming and she wants me to be awake for them. Or maybe it's something else, maybe there's something else I need to see. Something I won't like. I wonder if Irene is who I think she is. What if she's the bad one? What if she's working for the Crains? Could she be Toni's wife? I wonder if Toni has a wife. I wonder if Gabriel is really his son. I'm doing this to myself again. I'm making up scenarios in my head. What if she's just a nurse who's genuinely looking out for me? But who does that nowadays? Who really cares anymore?

She leans back into the chair and pulls up the paper to her face. I don't see her now, but I'm sure the glasses are still hanging from her neck. I pay no attention. I'm paralyzed to everything but my thoughts.

Irene shakes her paper again and I open my eyes a little. What are you doing, Irene? Why do you keep distracting me? Are you trying to make me open my eyes to take me away from the height of my senses? Are you trying to blind me from my thoughts? From finding out who did this?

She's getting up to leave.

'Sorry, Mr Jackson. Didn't mean to wake you again. Thank you for our little lunch date.'

Has an hour really passed? Has it been that long? I wait for her to disappear before I stick myself back into the darkness.

I won't let you do this, Irene. I've done this

before, I've walked down the road towards my goal, waving away all the flies and bees that had been hovering over me. I can't afford to do that now. I must pay attention, I need to think straight, I need to stop taking detours to the what-ifs, and instead, focus on the facts of what I did, how I did it, and how I ended up here.

I let out a slight sigh as she walks away and a meteor shoots through my chest aiming for my heart. I should have learnt by now not to breathe like that, but clearly, I don't learn from my lessons.

'Some wait around for the opportunity, taking the long way around to get there, and others take it, even if it's not theirs and it doesn't matter who they step on along the way. Light versus dark, heaven versus hell, good versus bad. When the opportunity is there, you take it, even if it's somebody else's, you take it and you make it yours.'

That's what Patrick told me after he got his director position at R.E.L. Bribery and corruption don't just work with the Crains. What's right and what's wrong doesn't matter anymore, you just take what you want and everyone around you will either go with it or fight back.

So that's what I decided to do when I found out what I did. I took that opportunity and I made it mine. Fuck Patrick. Fuck him and fuck the Crains.

CHAPTER **SIXTEEN**

I'm grounded to the truth of what you really are

Each breath is heavier, louder, as it grips on to those emotions, those truths that you buried long ago. It squeezes them out from your pores for everyone to see whilst hovering a thick blindfold over your eyes, placing you in the dark. But it's too transparent. Too controlling. Alcohol, it's too strong for mankind.

Four days ago

Come rain or shine, it was game on. Revenge. I had always considered it. I had always wanted it. Now I was able to serve it. I was able to serve the man who earned the aftermath of his desires through the name of karma. It would be a dish best served cold. Ice cold. But not until scouring his flesh against the heat of the flame. Not until his neck wrung limp against the sharpness of cold steel. This bully, this rapist, he was finally going to get what was coming to him. It was finally time to lay down the rat trap so he could feel the steel as it frees his soul so it can escape, and disappear. I stood in front of the mirror as my reflection ignited the fire within me.

'Uncle Kai, that's probably for you.'

Skye slumped down onto the couch accidentally knocking her knee onto the coffee table that was filled with sandwiches, crisps and sausages.

'I've got it.'

He was here. I'd gained his trust and it was time for the grand finale. The final stage of the plan. The plan that Toni and Vin hadn't filled me in on. All I had to do was invite Patrick to my home and drown his insides with alcohol, and everything else would sort itself out. They were confident that their plan was going to work, and so was I. Whatever their plan was.

'Wait, Kai.' Gabriel ran down the stairs like a galloping horse in battle. He stopped at the bottom of the stairs, catching his breath as he glared at me.

'Do you mind taking the dining room? Skye and I are going to watch a film.'

The mockery of being cast away from my own

living room by someone who was so much younger than me played on my mind but with Gabriel being the son of my boss, I had no option but to obey orders. Skye, Bella, Gabriel too, we came together under one umbrella, branded a family. Except this family was no longer mine, but Toni's.

'Thanks.'

I stared at Patrick standing in my porch, dressed up in his chinos and white polo shirt as if he were going somewhere a little more special than my home.

'I bought a few cans.' He raised his arms, showing off the eight pack that was hanging from each of them.

Nice. You're planning on getting wasted, makes my job easier. I moved out of the way, welcoming this rapist into my home for the first time.

'Come through, Patrick, straight into the dining room.' I ushered him in, my friend.

'The dining room is fine.'

I didn't know I'd given him an option. I sure didn't have one.

'Damn, Kai. I could eat, look at all this!' He hovered around the dining table where Skye had laid out some more snacks to keep us quiet as they watched their film in peace in the room next door.

'Don't mind if I do. Egg mayo, can't go wrong.'

He picked up a sandwich without waiting for me

to tell him to help himself. I assumed it was a respect thing, that he didn't have any. Not for me or my home. Or maybe he was comfortable around me. I wasn't sure, and I didn't care. This project was about to be over and I could finally be done with Patrick.

'I'll get you a cold drink, and stick these in the fridge.'

'Thanks for inviting me over. You're lucky. I didn't have anything planned for this weekend.'

He bit into his sandwich as a clump of egg slid out and onto the carpet. He moved forward towards a small sofa in the corner of the dining room, crushing the egg beneath his shoes.

He was like a flame. A flame that would consume whatever it pleased without a care. I hated him. I hated his obnoxious personality, his demeanour, everything. Him being around me only increased my impulse to feel the need to be aggressive towards him. And I would, anonymously inside my head. Inside my sickened mind that was fuelled with hate as I rode in the car that took me along the devil's path whilst my energy was focused on only one thing. Destruction.

After over twenty years of keeping up the act of 'friendship', after putting up with his passive-aggressive bullshit and covering up his sadistic acts of inhumanity among all those women, it was finally time to sprinkle bad luck over him and put an end to it all. It was my last task with Patrick and it was going to be so easy.

'Here we go.' Get this poison down you. I stared at him as I joined him on another small sofa beside a shelf filled with Skye's books, switching on a small TV in the corner of the room before passing the remote to my guest.

'Quite a cosy little set up you've got going on here, Kai. Not bad for a barman.'

He turned off the TV and placed the remote on the armrest beside him and I wondered whether he was here on business too.

Not bad for a barman? He was only into his first drink but his tongue was already prepped.

Soon, Patrick. Soon you'll get what's coming to you. I took a sip from my can as the cold sensation ran through my body, feeding the fire that was burning inside me. I am more than just a barman, Patrick. I am powerful. I am deadly. I want you to know just how dangerous I am. I want to warn you, you cannot disrespect me in my home. Soon, Patrick. Soon you will know.

I'd given him a cold, hard stare as the poison of hatred passed through my veins, surging through the sweetness of my blood turning it into saltwater. I was beginning to drown as all of his comments over twenty years seeped out from within the cracks that I had buried them in.

'You look exhausted, Kai! How about I go grab two more cans from the fridge for us, eh? Serve you for once.'

Exhausted I am. Exhausted from drowning in your presence. Go on now, Patrick. Yes, that's right. You serve me. You serve me while I sit and wait for Toni and Vin's plan to take effect. You serve me until I can watch the show take place in front of me. I've been waiting for this moment for a very long time, Patrick. You have no idea.

Today

Ivanova is walking through my space with her rattling trolley but she's not coming to me. I have my eyes closed but I can tell it's her by the sounds of her footsteps. They're heavy and she takes larger strides than Irene, who has short, stumpy legs yet it's Ivanova who does the stomping.

She walks out of Mr Kahele's space with her trolley. I assume she thinks I'm asleep because she hasn't made a sarcastic comment, but how can I sleep through this noise? Rattling trollies, beeping machines, patients being strangled to death.

I wonder whether I was supposed to know that. Whether I was supposed to hear him dying. And now I wonder why Ivanova and the other nurses couldn't hear Mr Martinez struggling to breathe. Why did no one hear him? Why did no one do anything? I wonder whether it was my paranoia or a hallucination. But it doesn't make sense. Mr Martinez did die that night. Irene had said so. Or at least, I think she did.

If Martinez was murdered, it was because he tried to save me. Which means the Crains must be involved. Which means Skye and Bella...Oh, God.

I write off that feeling. There is no way anything would happen to those girls. It's impossible. I can feel myself getting choked up and I can't swallow. I can't keep it in. I feel like I'm a bottle of fizz and someone has just slipped some Mentos inside me. I'm ready to explode but I don't know why. I don't know why I keep doing this to myself. I'm the creator of my own Mentos and I'm slipping them into my brain waiting for it to erupt and spill over until there's nothing left. Except there's never *nothing* left. I keep breaking the rules and working myself up through the words of other people that linger inside me, shaking it up with my own as it torments me silently. I don't even know what they're saying and my mind is filled with negatives.

Anger is a fucked up thing to have. Maybe that's why I'm here, maybe that last Mentos was too big.

I messed up. I was stupid and naïve, blinded by greed. I think maybe this trap to set Patrick up is really for me. When you only look down one road, you're blinded by what's behind you and on either side. I can't see them moving in, setting me up to close the game, but I'm sure that's what they're doing. They're setting me up.

I feel like I've been led down a path that's taken me right into the devil's home. Maybe I've always known this. I guess, sometimes your mind needs time to accept what your gut already knows. But it may be too late, I took too long. That's why I'm here, that's why the girls might be in danger. No.

Fuck, Ivanova. Why does her presence always do this to me? Nothing about this place is peaceful. I can't tell when one day starts and the other ends. These lights are always on, even at night and I can't see in the light, not how I used to.

Four days ago

'So, what's the deal with you? I've always wondered, why do you fuck those girls up the way you do?'

Five cans of beer and being in the comfort of my own home gave me the confidence to casually ask this rapist why he did what he did.

He passed me another can as a peal of nervous laughter left his mouth. I knew this sound well. I'd use it myself each time I spoke with Toni and Vin, or anyone else who made me wary of their company. I wondered what it was after all these years that made Patrick so wary of me.

'Sandwich? Sausages? Sausage-sandwich?' He took a plate, adding sausages between the bread of Skye's ready-made sandwiches. 'Tell me, sir, what may I get you? Or whatever it is that you waiters say.'

'I'm a barman, not a waiter.' A fountain of beer oozed from the top of the can as I opened it.

'Same thing.' He took a bite from his new sandwich and sat down on the sofa.

If only you knew who I was, Patrick, you would respect me more. I took a sip from the poison that fed my inner voice. I know you will tell me your secrets, Patrick. You can't hide anything from me. You're gearing yourself up for it, I can see it, all the bullshit with the sandwiches and sausages is just you building yourself up to tell me. Of all the years I've known you, I have picked up at least that much.

'So?' I took another sip from my poison, encouraging him to do the same.

'You know, Kai, women are fucked up.'

He sat back, into the sofa slouching on one side, spitting out breadcrumbs over his polo shirt as his glasses began to slide down his nose with each bite.

'When my mother fell down the stairs, she'd told

163

everyone that I pushed her. I didn't, but who'd believe a thirteen-year-old over an adult? My dad didn't for one.'

It was the first time he'd ever spoken of his personal life. I guess there's a feeling of comfort when you're in a house that feels like a home. It's like a big safety blanket, a warm, cosy one that wraps around you and hugs you tight enough to keep you safe, but loose enough to let you breathe. And I could see it. I could see Patrick breathe. For the first time, he was calm, comfortable, although a little intoxicated. He slid his glasses back onto the ridge of his nose.

'I didn't push her but she made that accusation. I used to get punished for all of the things she said I did. So…'

I felt sorry for him. The sadness in his voice and the look on his face as he turned away reminded me of that last day with Gracie in the garden. The day I should have listened.

'So I pushed her for real after she accused me of doing it. She cracked her rib on the way down and I kind of fucked her up a little and she was unable to live with us.'

I sat up in my seat, wide-eyed in disbelief as the world around me froze for a brief moment. Did he kill his mum? Was he a murderer as well as a rapist? Who was this man I had allowed into my home?

'Patrick, did…'

'I didn't murder my mum.' He read my mind. 'I wasn't to know she was ill. She was taken into care after that and there was just Dad and I left. He became obsessed with work and used to leave me with one of the parents from school until eight-ish every evening.' He'd taken a long sip from his can before lowering his head, studying the floral patterns that were laid out on the carpet beneath us.

'Their daughter was a few years younger than me. She'd claimed I did things to her. I didn't touch her but I got the blame for it. I was a teenager at the time and they punished me. The scars on my back and all the way down my legs, although no one can see them, I know they're there.'

He took another long swig of his beer and sat forward with his eyes now fixated on the sandwiches.

'There were no tests or anything. My dad did nothing to prove my innocence, just paid them off to stay quiet. He believed them over me.'

He moved further down into the sofa allowing himself to sink within it as the colour I was most familiar with began to sweep over his eyes.

'Dad was going to send me away to some sort of juvenile sanction for under sixteens. It was a six-week, hard-core confinement plan for kids with behavioural issues. Me? Behavioural issues? Not then. I couldn't be the only innocent kid there. You know what they would have done to me?'

He looked back down again and for a moment, I felt his pain. I felt his loneliness and his inability to cope with the shit that life had thrown at him.

'I gave myself something to be guilty of and...' He paused and wiped the crumbs from his top as they sprinkled over the flowers on the floor. 'I did it. I did it to someone else for real.'

He stared into the blank canvas of his polo shirt ashamed with what he'd admitted and I saw it. Remorse. Regret. He had raped somebody because he was accused of raping someone before he'd even done it. I didn't understand it. I didn't try to. Even if he'd given me his glasses, I'd never have seen it the way he did. But I did know it was wrong. It was wrong what they did to him. How they made him feel about himself. How their actions caused him to hit back the way he did. I understood at least that. I understood why he despised women the way he did and I felt sorry for him. He was just as pathetic as me. Weak and pathetic. The only difference between us was that he didn't do it for a living. He had to be numb. Out of touch with his emotions. Unlike me, who remained sober each time.

I was beginning to see who the real monster was as the sunlight beamed in through the window and onto my face.

'Say it.' He whispered, waiting for me to make a judgmental comment.

I didn't know what he wanted me to say. I wasn't going to attack a man who just admitted to having fallen victim to the occurrence of life even though what he did was fucked up. Who was I to judge? I was a killer.

'Another drink?' He smiled, accepting my offer and I could see the appreciation in his face as I accepted him for being nothing but human.

'Seeing as we're being so honest with each other, why are you still a barman?'

I should have known that was coming.

'Don't roll your eyes, mate. You know, years ago you wanted to work at the office with me.'

For the first time, it had felt as though we were having a real conversation. One that didn't feel so forced. We were having a conversation where I was able to get to know him and understand him better, with nothing to pass on to Toni and Vin in return.

'Why'd you settle, Kai?' Patrick looked up at me as he continued to steer the conversation away from him.

Settle. Was that the right word to use, to sum up what I did? I may have settled for the first paid job that came to me, but I didn't settle. Not before. Not when you look at the situation I was in. The situation at home, with a pregnant teenaged sister, and our financial state when they were born, the mess I was stuck with when Grace had died, and the shit I had to deal with when Mum was going crazy. I didn't settle. I did shit. Shit that most people wouldn't even think of. I took those kids on like they were my own and I did everything I could with what I had and more. I did shit. I got up and I worked harder than I should have for someone my age at the time. Every fucking day. Don't tell me I settled Patrick, don't you dare.

'A job's a job. Guess it was just easy money, especially when people like you shower me with those generous tips every day.' I smiled at him, raising my can. Take another sip, Patrick.

Just because he was in my home didn't mean we shared a friendship. It was business and I was simply working. I wasn't going to mess up this ordeal with the Crains, especially when the game was so close to completion. That sympathy I felt for him had been frozen. Iced over. Numbed.

'Let me get you another.' He'd eaten too many sandwiches and was sobering up too quickly. I needed to fulfil my task.

'Agh!' I hit my hip against the side of the table before stumbling to the ground and within seconds, Patrick was already by my side helping me up.

'I got you, mate. Grab a sandwich and sit back down. I'll get my drink.'

He walked me back to the sofa as though he'd been helping the elderly cross a busy road. I stumbled over my foot. Stop it, Kai. You can't mess this up. How was I drunker than him? Sandwiches. I needed to eat.

I jolted as he slammed two cans down on the table, realising I'd taken a quick nap.

'Well, this is a first!' He stared at me, as his lips stretched across his face with pride.

My eyes were heavy and I was just about able to keep them open. I needed to slow down.

'I need to catch up. No more sandwiches for me, mate. I want to be on your level.' He laughed as he took the last sip from his can before reaching out for the new one. 'The level you're at now, of course, not the one you were at a second ago when you were playing starfish on the floor.'

The clean and crisp sound of his can opening vibrated in my ears as I began to forget again, that this whole 'friendship' thing was purely business. He didn't seem too bad.

He'd gone through his fair share of bullshit, more than what he'd told me I'm sure. I guess he was just as human as I was. I guess we were both just trying to survive this thing called 'life'.

'Need a top-up?' Gabriel popped his head through the door. 'Skye's asking.'

Are you checking to see if Patrick's drunk,

Gabriel? Do you think I can't get the job done? Or is it a warning for me? You being here, is it a reminder, to tell me not to get comfortable in my home? Do you want me to sober up, Gabriel? Is that what you want? Is this part of the plan? Who are you checking in on, Gabriel? Me, or Patrick?

'We're good thanks.' I slurred as Patrick sniggered in the corner of the sofa like a school kid.

'Your son? Didn't know you had kids.' Patrick waited for Gabriel to leave the room and took a bigger, longer swig from his can.

Why are you so nervous, Patrick? Are you working with them too? I felt a thick, dark cloud wash over my eyes as Gabriel's presence awoke my inner voice. That short feeling of friendship disappeared, and this time for good.

'Nieces' boyfriend.' I bit into my sandwich. I didn't want to talk about the twins, not to him.

He nodded, as he took another long sip.

I'm grounded to the truth of what you really are, Patrick. You can't fool me. No way, not in my house. Don't get too comfortable.

I watched him, walking from the sofa to the table, to the kitchen and back, strutting around in my home as if it was his, as if he was welcome. This was business. Strictly business. I wanted him to know that.

'Drink up, I'm going to get out the whisky.' I

rammed another sandwich down my throat on my way to the cabinet across the room and took out a bottle of whisky and two glasses.

One after the next, he drank the poison I poured out for him as he allowed for it to intoxicate his entire body.

The tables were about to turn and revenge was going to be sweet. Drink up, Patrick.

CHAPTER **SEVENTEEN**

All that is certain in life, is death

We'll burn each other until the entire planet turns to nothing but ashes, leaving not even the smallest fragment of goodness behind.

Today

The sound of beeping awakens me from my sleep. The nurses are rushing towards Mr Kahele's space and it seems like he may be the next to leave. I can just about make out Ivanova'a silhouette before she disappears behind the curtain as though she's in some kind of magic show. For a second, I think this may be an ugly trick that they're all playing in this game I know nothing about. I don't want to play and I feel like I'm waiting in line behind Mr Kahele to fall victim to these nurses like Martinez.

I hear Kahele, gasping for air as though a thief is stealing it from his lungs. Short, stumpy puffs replace his wheezing and I imagine he's being choked. I wonder if it's them. I wonder if it's Ivanova. His gasps are becoming muted as I recall the same with Martinez and I'm trying to picture what's going on next door.

There are three or four nurses in there with him, maybe more. There's a lot of movement and I don't feel comfortable. The beeping is consistent but the shuffling seems to be coming to a stop. I'm not sure, but I think Mr Kahele has just died. There's a sudden pause around me as everyone turns still, frozen to their spot. It's dead silent and I can feel something creeping into my space although there's nobody here. I know for sure he's dead, I know this feeling.

Despite all the souls I have watched disappear from the eyes of those I have killed, despite hearing so many take their final breath once their heart has taken its last beat, and despite all the times I have walked away from the piles of meat that once carried a soul, the silence that followed has always lingered, coming in slowly before surging into my eardrums and deafening me. It was the same when I saw Grace's dead body. That deadly silence. That moment when the world stops, but carries on. Life. Death. Two down. Two more to go.

They're all leaving one by one, sneaking out like shadows in the night, leaving me with no one but Mr Kahele's dead body, and this giant man in a coma. I wonder how long he's been here. I wonder if, like me, he can hear everyone dying around him.

The hairs over my body stand tall as the shadows in this room around me grow taller, sucking me into a forest that wasn't there before. I'm in the dark, and I can see it. I can see that the lights have been dimmed for the first time since I've been here. And I can see that they're hiding something from me. There is someone else in there with Mr Kahele. I just know it.

Stop it, Kai. Stop it, just stop it. I'm not doing this. I can't do this. I won't let my mind wander into the thickness of the forest. I can't. I can't be lurking amongst those creatures that strive off the darkness, not anymore. I can't do it. I can't hide within those trees especially if the trees are against me. I won't let myself wander in there, otherwise, I'll never find my way out.

Four days ago

'Now, this is more like it.'

Patrick was slumped across the side of the sofa,

leaning into the armrest almost hanging off the edge. His head wobbled like a nodding toy dog in the back of a car while the rest of his body swayed as though he were travelling on a ship in the midst of a storm. But he wasn't at sea, he was in my house about to be seasick all over my floral carpet. Mum's floral carpet.

I glared at him, staring him out as he began to swallow his saliva as an attempt to stop himself from vomiting. He leaned back into the sofa and closed the curtains of his eyelids as I continued to watch him. Who are you, Patrick? How do you embrace the comfort of being in my home? This isn't your usual environment. There are no distractions here. No women, noise or music. Yet you're at peace in my home, more relaxed than usual. What's going on in there, in that mind of yours? Do you think you're safe here? Do you think I'm your friend? You're not so smart now are you, Patrick? You've let your guard down. It can't protect you here, not even if it was tougher than the shield of a superhero. Tell me, Patrick, after doing what you do, how do you sleep so…human?

The cracks are easier to see when someone's asleep, eyes closed and vulnerable. Patrick had taken off his mask. I could see his face, his worries, his sorrows. I could see it all through the flaws on his skin. I could see beyond the thickness of this layer that he'd masked himself in. I could see *him*. Innocence leaked through his pores although he was guilty. He was broken. A broken man who only knew how to brush alcohol and money over his imperfections. The harder I looked the more I saw.

He had dozed off intoxicated with the poison I made him drink. I'd taken away his shield and now I could see him for what he really was. Weak, pathetic and empty. Just like me. Watching him felt no different from looking in the mirror. He was just as lost as I was and his life was just as fucked up as mine. We were both the same. Both the same but different. But just so fucking the same.

I screamed through the silence as my insides tightened and I knew I was going to be sick with guilt. Blame worked its way around my body reminding me that this man sleeping on my sofa let himself become vulnerable in my home because he believed I was harmless. Because he believed I was his friend. I was going to betray him and possibly get him killed. I had to tell him the truth. I had to.

Wake up, Patrick. I need to tell you something.

'Damn, Kai.' Gabriel's head peered through the door again. 'Don't mind me, I'm just filling up on snacks for Skye. He good?'

Gabriel strolled through the dining room and into the kitchen whilst my gut began to clench, sending me signals I didn't want.

You're not here to 'fill up on snacks,' are you, Gabriel? You're wondering why we've gone silent. You're working with your dad. You have no business with my niece, do you, Gabriel? You're a spy. Aren't you, Gabriel? I was sure of it. Either way, I took it as a warning to stick with the plan.

'He's good.' I raised my voice but not enough for him to hear me from where he was.

He's good now but not for long, Gabriel. Not if your dad has anything to do with it. I had too much at stake, too much to lose. Better Patrick than me. Better Patrick than the girls.

I moved away from the sofa to join Gabriel in the kitchen. I was as hungry as I was sober.

'…According to plan. He's aslee…'

Gabriel spun around faster than a tornado as the flooring creaked beneath my feet. Confirmed. He was there on business. He slid his phone into his pocket as though it was never in his hands, as though he was never whispering into it, as though he wasn't making that call, that call to update his master on Patrick's physical state.

'Hungry?' I headed over to the cupboard and took out a bag of pasta as if I'd heard nothing.

He declined my offer as he held back his shoulders, standing up tall, threatening me with his posture and height as he strolled out of the kitchen acting like a tiger that had just made a kill. I didn't care. I was following orders, remaining committed to the Crains, and as long as I did that, the girls would be safe.

I drew the curtains over the fake fluorescent lighting from the street-lamps outside.

'How have you still got your kidneys?' I stabbed my fork into two pasta shells that I'd drowned in tomato sauce as Patrick took a long sip of his beer.

'I aim to stay in the state I'm in, Kai. I'll sleep well tonight.' He pushed up his glasses as they attempted to escape.

So that's your secret. That's why you drink so much. That's how you sleep like you're human. Alcohol, it's your escape from whatever demons you have inside your head like the drugs were for Grace. I wonder, what is mine?

'Gonna show me around your palace before I leave, sir?' Patrick placed his empty bowl on the table opposite him and as if on cue, Gabriel walked in, followed by Skye and Bella.

'We're going to have dinner now, so feel free to move into the next room.' Skye looked over at me concerned about this drunken man I was babysitting.

'He's good. He's just about to leave anyway.' I assured her.

'After you've given him a tour of the palace.'

Gabriel smirked as he walked into the kitchen. I knew there was more to it but like everything else in my life, I ignored it.

Patrick said nothing as he glared down at his can of beer that he cradled in his hands.

That's right, Patrick, keep looking down. Don't you dare look up at my girls.

'Well, this is my living room. Not much to it really.' He stumbled as he looked around.

There were two three-seater sofas and an armchair facing a TV in the corner of the room. A large mirror stood tall on the wall where our fireplace used to be, and a shelf underneath that was home to a range of little photos of Mum, Grace and myself when we were younger, and Skye and Bella too. Opposite that were French doors overlooking into the long garden which had been paved down to the apple tree that stood at the end where Grace had been buried. We'd kept everything plain and simple. The walls were painted white all over, and the carpets were grey throughout the entire house except in the dining room where we'd kept Mum's floral carpet in her memory.

I watched him glance across the shelf, stumbling towards it, still intoxicated. He stopped to pick up a photo of Grace and held it closer to his face.

Get away from my dead sister you rapist. I am

not comfortable with you in my home. I am not comfortable with you looking at these photos. Looking at, checking out, perving, whatever it is you're doing. Put it down.

'Patrick, how about the garden?' I edged towards the French doors.

'Wait. I think I know this chick.' He slurred a little on his words but I made out what he was saying. 'How do *you* know her?'

How the fuck did you know Grace? I moved towards him to usher him away from the photos and out of my home. There was no way he knew her, she was dead.

'I went to school with her. Fuck, she…'

I looked at him and saw the light fade from his eyes as we both came to understand what he was about to admit. I needed to be sure. 'Grace?' I walked towards him.

'Grace.' He whispered back, dropping his head as low as he could hold it. 'How do you know her?'

I could feel something inside my body ignite as it began to burn with rage but I needed to be sure.

'What happened, Patrick?' My cheeks, my nose, my shoulders, I could feel myself flaring up, getting ready to explode like fireworks but I couldn't show him. I needed to know if it was *that*.

'I'm sorry.' He stepped back upon seeing my face and moved as though preparing himself to escape out the door and out of the house like the coward that he was.

I moved fast towards him and he stepped back, stumbling against the side of the shelf. Her photo fell from his hands as he headed toward the door but I got to him first. I grabbed him by his hair and dragged him back to the shelf. He was weak and filled with alcohol, making it easier for me to kill him.

'What did you do, Patrick?' I smacked his head against the shelf as his glasses flung from his face. I turned him towards me as the fingers of my free hand wrapped around his neck and squeezed tight enough to hear him choke.

'Patrick!' The sound of death wrapped around my weak, quiet voice as it rumbled out of me like an angry tornado. 'What did you do?' I knew I was going to kill him. The storm had entered the room.

'I told you, Kai.' I could hear the remorse in his voice as tears rolled down his face. He struggled to speak as I clenched my fingers into his skin. I let go, throwing him against the mirror as though he were a javelin. I was burning. My fire had been ignited and I was the biggest flame in the room.

'Grace! I need to speak to her. I need to tell her I'm sorry.' I grabbed him by his hair again and slammed his head against the shelf.

He yelled out in pain, calling for Grace. How

dare you say her name. How fucking dare you? I moved his head back and smashed it against the shelf again as the glass from the photos pierced into his skin.

'*You* don't say her name!' I could see in Patrick's face, that he was terrified. Terrified of me.

'Kai!' He shouted out for me to stop as I pulled his head back, ready to smash his face into his reflection.

'She's dead.' I slammed his head into the mirror as the weight of his arms pulled the shelf off the wall. 'You killed her!'

I tightened my grip on the back of his head and slammed his face into the mirror, continuously like a champion boxer in a ring without a referee.

Words refused to leave my mouth but I wanted to tell him, I wanted to tell him over and over that he killed my sister, he got her pregnant, he raped her, he killed her.

Rage flooded within me and all I wanted was to see his blood smeared across the white walls of my home. The flames were burning violently, burning my soul with each strike of Patrick's head to the glass. Die, Patrick. Blood splattered from his face and onto the mirror and walls. Die. He'd been crying, begging me to stop but I couldn't. I couldn't stop. His screams made it worse, fuelling my anger like gasoline to my fire. Glass few across the room like the flickering sparks of the devil's flames. Fuck! He *raped* Grace!

Rage got the worst of me and the more he cried out the more I carried on banging his head against the shards of broken glass, letting it tear into his skin. I wanted to smash his skull open and rupture his brain, I wanted him to know exactly what he did to my family, to me. I wanted him to suffer the worst possible form of torture. He deserved to die.

'She's dead because of you!' I couldn't stop. I was a burning fire and I was ready to turn him into ashes. I slammed his head against the mirror. My sister was *raped*. Grace was raped. My Gracie.

The sounds of glass shattering turned into thuds as I slammed his head into the backing of the mirror. There was a hurricane inside me demanding to be set free. This fucker, this scum had raped my sister. This man was the father of my nieces. He was in my house, under my roof, drinking with me, eating with me. Patrick!

My emptiness was filled with purpose and my thoughts refused to travel from within me as I became numb to any feeling or emotion other than the need to destroy him. This murderous rapist was heavy and limp as I moved his head back from the wall. I swung my arm, positioning myself for his destruction, throwing every bit of energy I had left into the tips of my knuckles before attempting to shatter his skull into tiny pieces.

I don't know if I did it. I don't remember. But something warm began to run down the back of my head and suddenly it all went black.

CHAPTER **EIGHTEEN**

I didn't have the alpha gene, but I was the alpha

The blackness nurtures all but one of his senses whilst robbing the other. Place a blindfold over the eyes of a wolf but he'll know you're coming. He can feel the sound of the leaves crackling beneath your feet, and he can smell the thick scent of the earth as it rises into the atmosphere. He'll know you're coming, even if he can't see.

I faded into unconsciousness, with the ears of the wolf.

Four days ago

'Uncle Kai?' Skye cradled me on the floor of our living room. 'He's waking up, B.'

The touch of Bella's hand over mine made me

185

feel human again as Skye brushed her hands over my head.

'Uncle Kai, are you okay?' She sounded like her mother. I kept my eyes closed and relaxed into the floor imagining Gracie nursing me like she did when we were kids.

'I'm sorry, Uncle Kai.' A drop of saltwater trickled onto my face. 'G was afraid you were going to kill that man, so he had to stop you.'

Skye's voice was just as soft as Grace's but her words stung as the reality of what had happened started to come back to me.

We need to get out of here. You need to hide somewhere, go someplace safe, both of you. Go. I tried to move. Let me deal with this. Let me find Patrick. Let me kill him. I couldn't get up.

'Skye, you think he's got concussion or trauma or something? He doesn't look right.' Bella's arms wrapped around me as she forced me back down to the floor.

'Where…' I began to open my eyes as Skye wiped away her tears.

'Uncle Kai, can you hear me?'

I can hear you, Bella, I can hear you.

'Where…'

'What is it? What are you trying to say? Where is what, Uncle Kai?'

Where is Gabriel? He hit me hard and I could

tell it wasn't the first time he'd hit a man. I could tell he wanted to do more than just stop me.

'Where is he?'

'They're gone now, don't worry. G took him. He called Toni and they went.'

Fuck.

'He said you're not safe. You might have messed up their plan or something. What have you done?'

The sound of Skye's phone vibrating against the wood from the table took her away from me.

'It's G.' She moved into the dining room as the shards of glass from the mirror crackled beneath her shoes.

'Are you feeling okay?' Fear glazed over Bella's pupils and I knew she was scared for my wellbeing.

'I'm fine.' I lied. I was far from feeling fine. My actions had put these girls in danger and I was in no position to fix it.

'I don't know how you got into this mess, Uncle Kai.' Skye came back. 'But G says you're in a lot of trouble. He said we need to get you somewhere where they can't find you.'

She was trying not to panic but I could hear the jumpiness in her voice, she was just as afraid for me as I was for them.

'I'm taking you to one of his garages. I know where it is. Can you get up? Can you walk?'

I assumed Gabriel had only told her a small

percentage of how much trouble I was actually in.

'Skye, what are you saying?' The colour from Bella's face had been stolen as a layer of pale peach brushed over her. I couldn't help but blame myself.

'Come on, we don't have time.' Skye tapped into her phone screen whilst ushering Bella to get up. 'G said we need to hurry. I know where his garage is. I have the keys. The cab should be here any minute.'

'Patrick…' I couldn't help but wonder what they'd done with Patrick.

'It's okay, Uncle Kai. He's gone.' Bella rubbed her hand gently over my forehead.

'He has to die.' I moved back up off the floor.

'Uncle Kai, seriously, we don't have time for this. Bella, get him up, I'll get him some water and pack some food. We need to move.'

I knew they were coming for me. They were coming for me like hunters in the night. Robbing me of my sanity, draining my body of warmth, weaving paranoia into fragments of my reality, and leaving me out there, for my soul to wander. Toni, Vin and probably Gabriel too - the killers of the night, they were coming for me.

I messed up. I almost killed Patrick and right at the end of their plan, whatever their plan was. He was the cause of my life being the way it was and I had to make him pay for his sins. Take him down like a silver wolf fighting for his pack. I didn't have that alpha gene, but I was the alpha, especially when it came to my girls.

'It's here.' Skye had a bag filled with drinks and snacks in her hands and I wondered how she managed to fill it up so quickly as we moved out of the house and into the cab.

I sat in the back, slipping in and out of sleep as I lay my head against the window. Bella squeezed my hand and I squeezed hers back as I recalled the last time I held her hand, twenty-three years ago when they were seven years old, in the car on the way to Grace's funeral. And now I was going to mine.

'Are you both staying with me?' I looked up to Skye who had been seated in the front with her eyes glued to the map on her phone, making sure the driver was moving in the right direction.

'No, just you. But I'll be back again tomorrow.' Her eyes were still fixated on her phone.

'You'll be okay.' Bella squeezed my hand again.

It didn't make any sense. Why wouldn't Gabriel keep Skye and Bella in hiding too? He knew how the Crains worked. Surely he knew that my family would be at risk? Are they under your protection, Gabriel? Please keep them safe. Maybe we were a part of their *family* after all. But I was the alpha. I had to protect my pack.

Stay with me. Please. Skye, Bella, I need you to stay with me. Please.

It made all the sense in the world for them to stay with me, but I couldn't do it. I was a wolf without a howl. I had no voice. I was muted. I sat there in silence, holding on to Bella's hands for the last time.

We slowed down as I woke to see a row of garages just off the main road. The reflection of two rather large eyes peered up at me from the rearview mirror as the driver glared at me. It was Mr Kahele.

CHAPTER **NINETEEN**

There's always that thing, that thing called hope

If you're going to raise an angel only to stick him in hell, don't expect him not to pick up the devilish behaviours of the demons along the way.

Today

When you're done with being used, you become desperate to fight back and it doesn't matter how far you go, as long as you go. It's like a bomb that's ticking inside you and the longer you keep it in, the louder the explosion and the greater the damage.

I did things that made my world so much darker than it was before, so dark that even lightning wouldn't dare strike. I was a bird trapped inside a cage that I thought I'd been released from, still confined and limited to where I could fly. I'd been holding up my umbrella to avoid the rain but I never stopped the rain from falling. And because of me, we drowned. We. Me, Mum, Skye, Bella. I let this happen. Nobody else.

I guess when you go through shit, you pick up some inhumane survival tactics on the way. A bee stings when it feels threatened. A lion hunts when hungry. Humans, we survive differently. We numb those empty feelings, we revert to anger and hatred. We block out remorse because we no longer want to care. It's an escape of some sort, to hide the scars formed through the trauma we've faced after long periods of trying to deal with the bouts of bullshit in the right way. We betray ourselves, we lose our values, and worse, we forget who we are.

I can't help but question the person I've become. Maybe I'm weak, or maybe I'm just broken. Really broken. I wonder how long I've been broken for. These thoughts in my head tell me I've been drowning since forever and I can only assume I had been crushed by the weight of the waters a long time ago.

You'd think a man can't break, or at least you're taught to believe it. We're strong, we were made that way. The strength, the power, how would we break? We don't self-destruct, we aren't supposed to. You hear those stories of single mums struggling to make ends meet, and that's okay. But a single man taking care of children? Washing, cooking, cleaning, working? We exist, and we have bad days too. We do. We all do. I wish Mum had shown me that it was okay. Okay to be a man and not be okay. I didn't know, but I wish I did. I wish they all knew. But they didn't.

I focused so much on my conscious mind that I forgot about the one beneath it, the one that wanted to talk but could only whisper. I'd suffocate those whispers and I'd feed the silence, but it was still there, hidden but not discreet as it pierced my insides with the sharpness of its thorns, growing inside me within the darkness of my soul. I continued to pretend it wasn't there, that I was okay. Because everyone else's opinions, although they shouldn't matter, they did. They did and it made all the fucking difference.

It's like floating on a boat in the middle of the ocean until someone's words pierce a hole through the bottom and you're left sinking amongst the waves with an anchor wrapped tightly around your legs. It clings to you and pulls you down deeper into the darkness as the rain pours heavily over you. No matter how hard you move like it's not there, the destruction inside you will remind you of its presence. The rain will keep pouring and you'll drown. We all will. Or we won't. There's always that thing, that thing called *hope*. You just have to hope it's not too late. Hope. Dangling a life float to a drowning man with no intention of saving him. You give yourself hope, only to know you're going to die anyway.

When did I invite the demons in? When did they knock on my door? Their disguises are too good, and I'm too gullible. Or maybe I'm just stupid.

I sink back into the pillow and run my fingers over the photo of Skye and Bella. My only two remaining members of the family have decided I'm not worthy of their time despite knowing I've spent the past thirty years giving them mine. I guess I didn't do enough for them to love me. But it's not their fault. I gave those girls everything I possibly could only to leave them to deal with the mess that I'd created. I'd picked up my angels, and I'd placed them in hell.

'Good evening, Mr Jackson.' Ivanova seems a little disgruntled as she interrupts me from my moment of peace.

I wonder, why do I keep thinking of this as something that brings me peace? These thoughts have made me feel far from peaceful, yet somehow, this is the most at peace I have been since I was eighteen.

I look at Ivanova but she's not paying attention.

She's looking over at Mr Kahele's empty bed whilst injecting morphine into my body. Her face falls a little and I'm beginning to doubt whether she killed him after all. I wonder if she'll care when I'm gone. But I guess, if I didn't care about myself, why would anybody else?

'That's two empty beds now. I wonder who'll be next.' Ivanova smiles at me and walks away.

That wasn't friendly. That was fucked up. Why did you say that? Am I getting too comfortable with dying that you needed to bring me back to life? Bring me back to life only so you can kill me later, in your own way, the Crain way?

I feel the blood drain from my face and it's beginning to feel tight. Did she just give me some information on Skye and Bella? Were those two beds for them? Is that what she was getting at? Is that what she meant? Next where, Ivanova? Next to come in here or next for you to strangle to death? Because I'm sure Kahele didn't die without help, and neither did Martinez.

I hate this. I hate this game. I hate being in here. I hate not being able to speak. I hate this alone time. I hate thinking and I hate how it's making me feel. I hate these questions, these assumptions, I hate everything. I hate it, I hate it all. That Ivanova, I know for sure is working for the Crains. Maybe they all are. I had Martinez in here, who tried to save me, and Kahele, the cab driver. How did he even get in here? I don't remember. This can't be right. Did everyone in this room have some sort of relation to the Crains? I wonder, who is this guy in a coma? He is huge and I don't recall working with anyone as tall and big as him. I'm drifting a little and I don't know what Ivanova has given me but it's making me feel drowsy. I don't know if I'm in a hospital. Maybe this room is owned by the Crains. Maybe they caught me and I don't remember. Could that be Gabriel in that bed? It doesn't look like him. Patrick? It can't be.

I feel a little disgusted in myself for settling on believing this was a hospital. I should know better. I should know all about illusions and deception. I should know all about tricks and scams, and dishonesty and misconceptions. I've experienced it enough. Why didn't I pick this up before?

Disgust and fear are whirling inside me like a tornado, throwing out any peace I had felt before. That fear, that kind you have when you can't do anything but you need to do something, it's whirling around inside me, trashing my guts and turning my organs into collateral damage. My chest is getting tight again and I can feel the pain from the rod. She didn't give me morphine. This pain is too much. I know nothing will help the situation I'm in, the situation I've put myself in. The situation I've put the girls in.

I can't do shit to help Skye and Bella because I can't do shit to help me. I close my eyes. Fuck this.

Four days ago

'Uncle Kai, you'll be safe here, okay? We'll be back in the morning with G, he'll help. I promise.'

Bella was certain but I wasn't so sure. She didn't know how dangerous this situation was. The situation I'd put them in.

They placed me on a thin blanket on the floor as though I were a dog and I felt like one too. Not the strong, beasty kind, but more like a Chihuahua. Tiny and small.

'Get some rest now, we'll see you tomorrow, okay? I love you, Uncle Kai.'

I watched as they walked away from me, as they left me there on the dampness of the garage floor with nothing but a bag of food, a torch-light and some batteries.

No, Gabriel. I won't stay here sitting in your trap. You keep your batteries. I don't plan on staying here for long. I have my own plan. I have my own mission. My own Project Patrick.

'I love you too, girls.' Darkness hit me the moment the shutter slammed closed and suddenly, the pain in my head had awoken.

Whatever it was that Gabriel had used to save Patrick was sufficient enough to inflict the right amount of pain onto me to send me a message, telling me that he wasn't just stopping me from destroying Patrick. It was to stop me from running. It was a message of revenge. He had *my* girls bring me to his garage and lock me up in this cage like an animal. But I have my plan, Gabriel. First, it will be Patrick, and then it will be you.

I felt the warmth of my blood dripping down the back of my head telling me otherwise. It was dark and cold as I slipped in and out of sleep, turning my mind to nothing but blackness.

You don't become aligned with your true emotions until you're left with nothing but pitch black, when you've fallen deep into the darkness, to the lowest you can go, right down beyond the flames of hell, and further. When I was alone and in the darkness of the shadows, when I was truly on my own in the garage that night, I realised how weak I was. My arms had been holding up the roof for so long that my body and bones had become worn, fragile and were ready to cave in. I needed help. I needed help a long time ago.

It's like what the flight attendants say before a plane takes off, fix your own mask before fixing someone else's. I could see then that I'd spent my entire life running up and down a plane that was crashing, making sure everyone else had their masks on before putting on my own, all whilst trying to fly this plane and keeping it from going down. I had lost the way and I was too proud to ask for directions. I ended up floating deeper towards the thickness of a forest that bore only Manchineels - the trees of poison. Death was where I was headed, I just didn't know it then.

Bitter tears of anger, failure and disappointment filled my eyes but refused to leave me. I'd fucked up so hard that it was too late for me to answer this wake-up call. I had walked so far into the forest and dug myself a ditch so deep, that not only was I unable to climb out, but there was nobody around to hear me, nobody willing to pull me from this grave.

CHAPTER **TWENTY**

Talking. It's important and I wish I fucking did it

'Life can get you in so many ways, Kai. It's way too deep for me to describe it. People come into your life with different purposes and some of those purposes won't be for the good. They'll try to break you and broken leads to destruction. God, He doesn't destroy. He builds. Stay with Him, and don't break. Don't ever break, Kai.'

It makes sense to me now, why Gracie spoke to me the way she did. The words she used, the strength she pretended to have. She needed to hear those words. She needed reassurance after what Patrick had done to her. She was breaking, talking herself into being strong. She was just as damaged as I was. But Gracie, didn't you know? Sometimes you have to break so you can rebuild yourself. Sometimes you have to walk down to the darkest of places, into the pitch black. That's where your wings grow, Gracie, that's when you rise. You gave up, Grace. You destroyed yourself, and us too.

God, I love you. I close my eyes and hear her whisper to me as I remind myself that she loves me too. You shouldn't have left like that, you shouldn't have gone. Your kids needed you, I needed you. I'm sorry, Grace. You needed me too, I wish I had known. I wish you would have spoken to me, maybe I would have spoken to you too. We could have helped each other, Gracie. Talking. It's important and I wish I fucking did it.

Four days ago

I woke up in the darkness of the garage unsure of how long I had been there. I forced myself to sit up as a pool of dried blood lay where my head had been.

The light from my torch was aimed towards the shutter as I sat and stared at my way out. The sheet of metal was moving side to side, dancing with the rain that fell heavily outside. I moved the torch around the room. Garden tools were stacked neatly against the wall beside me as they too danced along with the sounds of the rain.

I wondered whether I'd been drugged or whether gas was being released into the garage. Everything was dancing, swaying around me, mocking me as they celebrated my defeat. I watched them move like flames as their shadows crept around me, moving closer towards me as I placed my torch over them, capturing each of them under the light from my spell.

Maybe I was still intoxicated with alcohol and rage. I guess paranoia gets the worst of you when you're down and vulnerable.

I moved the torch back towards the shutter as I watched the puddles seeping in like ghosts as they edged closer towards me. It was like being in a horror film except this was real.

I was fueled with hatred and revenge was my only option. Those thoughts, those feelings, they crushed my soul. I was a broken man with one thing on my mind. Murder. I couldn't sit and wait, I couldn't do it. I was sure Skye and Bella would be protected. Why else weren't they made to hide out with me? Whatever Gabriel's plan was, it included their protection. I knew deep down he felt something for Skye. I knew he did. Or at least that's what I kept telling myself.

I pushed every bit of energy I had left into my legs as I began to stand, floating on this magic, blood-stained carpet.

I moved my torch back to the garden tools.

'This isn't your garage, is it Gabriel? You don't do gardening, do you?'

I heard the sound of my voice as it shrivelled out of me, reminding me I was alone and weak.

Was I in a garage? I looked back to the pool of dried blood I'd been lying on and wondered if it was mine. Was I in a torture chamber? Were these tools meant for me? For my punishment? I didn't want to hang around to find out. I grabbed a pair of large hedge cutters from the wall and made my way over to the centre of the shutters, jacking my way into the lock until I heard it cling open. My escape was just about to begin but my plan to kill Patrick hadn't even started.

Two bright lights blinded me as soon as I pushed up the shutters. I stumbled over, fighting to pull it back down but something was in the way, jamming it at the other end. I tried to make out the face within the silhouette of the person who was refusing to let me lock myself in but I couldn't see. Two other silhouettes stepped out from the back of the car. That's three against one. I moved fast towards the wall of weapons, grabbing hold of a hammer before running back towards my exit, noticing a metal rod that had slipped and wedged itself beneath the shutter. Luck was on my side—it wasn't a person holding up the shutters. There were only two of them. Two against one. Come on, Kai. I tumbled towards the headlights as they continued to blind me. The two figures continued to walk towards me, shouting but their voices were drowned from the sound of the engine roaring over the showers that fell from the sky. Everything was blurry. They were angry, and they were coming for me.

I had to get out. I made my getaway and moved out of the garage, running fast towards the road until something struck my back, throwing me to the floor. I could taste the sweetness of the blood that spilled from my mouth as my breathing became harder. My chest pounded as I looked down at the pool of red that seeped through my shirt, surrounding the spear that had been professionally anchored into me.

The screams of a gunshot had awoken me from my unconsciousness. I tried to turn back but I couldn't see who it was. Another scream shot into the air and couldn't tell whether someone was firing at me, or someone else. I wasn't alone, someone was on my side. I dragged myself onto the road using the remaining bit of energy I had left in me until I stood there, leaning forward as though I was heaving, holding this shaft that had torn into my skin and through my muscles. I remained there, waiting to be shot. Waiting to die. And then I saw the light.

'What the…!' A voice yelled over me as the gunshots continued to scream through the air. 'Let's get you away from here. This is gonna hurt.'

I tried to scream but the sound refused to leave my body as my throat filled with blood. The pain was excruciating but the shots that followed were just as bad as they boomed through the air like thunder. The man heaved me into the back of his car with my body hovering between the front and back seats.

'They're pissed at you. What did you do?'

Surely he didn't expect me to answer. The sound of another gunshot screamed into my ears and I knew I was being pursued.

'What have I gotten myself into?' The man swerved sharply as he pushed down on the accelerator. My insides exploded with every turn he took and I knew, I knew I was going to die.

'Hang in there, old man. Not long to go, stay with me now.'

I passed out.

The sound of glass shattering took me away from my sleep, in time for me to hear another bullet scream through the air scraping across Martinez' shoulder, and another into his head as we crashed outside the hospital.

'He's losing a lot of blood.'

Flashes of light whizzed passed me as the paramedics wheeled me into the hospital. And that was the last thing I remember until I came out of the theatre and woke up in this room with three other men.

CHAPTER **TWENTY-ONE**

Who asks for help anymore?

Sometimes the answers are there, right in front of you, neatly wrapped inside a shiny piece of paper, presented to you inside a little box. You had it all along, you knew the answers. But you asked for help anyway. You asked someone to open the box, to unwrap the truths, trusting them to read it. You took hold of the devil's hand and you walked with him while he opened this parcel, while he held this shiny piece of paper into your eyes, blinding you from seeing what you already knew.

Today

Irene is walking into my space carrying her genuine smile like she always does. I don't know why, but I feel like reaching out to her. I'm becoming weak in here and for the first time in a long time, I feel as though I need love. I need someone to love me and take care of me. I see in Irene's eyes that she cares. The softness of her face and the way she's so relaxed around me makes me feel comfortable around her too. I can feel her kindness and somehow, I know she's on my side.

'Good morning, Mr Jackson.' She plays around with the monitor beside my bed.

I let myself relax a little and show her a smile. She smiles back. I've decided to take off my mask, just for a little while. I need to know if the girls are okay. I know she knows. I know she'll tell me.

'Mr Jackson,' she comes close and places her hand over mine. 'You know you need to keep that on, okay?' She moves my hand away from my mask and places it gently by my sides before securing the mask back on to my face again. Her hands are as warm as her smile and I feel soothed by her presence, but I'm also becoming slightly wary of her again. Why won't you let me speak, Irene? What is it that I could say wrong?

She winks at me and I wonder whether she's telling me not to worry, that they're okay, or that she's also playing a part in this game I know nothing about.

'You have a visitor, Mr Jackson.' Irene is already

looking at me as I glare at her, wide-eyed. 'Oh no, don't worry.'

She can read me well. I'm wondering whether Toni and Vin have come to finish the job.

'Haven't you been wanting someone to visit all this time?' I look at her and she seems pleased to share this news with me. My stomach fills with butterflies. I knew they'd come. I knew it. I feel my insides fluttering around as excitement surrounds me. The girls have come. Irene smiles again. She can see it in my eyes and I can see it in hers. She's real. She's happy for me. She's on my side.

'But it's not visiting hours yet, so we've asked him to come back at eleven.'

I sink into my bed. Him? What? What about Skye and Bella? Who is this 'him' that she's referring to? Coldness fills the room, biting at my skin and I can't help but think I will die next. Did Ivanova know that already? Is that what she meant last night about who was next? Did Irene know too? Fuck. Did Irene intentionally make me think my girls were here only to take that away from me? Is she one of them? Is she working with the Crains like Ivanova?

I need to get out. I'm in a car speeding along a bumpy road, heading far into the horizon with the girls in tow. But I'm not the one driving. I can't control it and I'm about to crash.

My chest is feeling heavier than a heart that's soaked in guilt, and it itches. I feel as though the incisions from my surgery are beginning to heal yet the pain is still there. Those cuts, those scars. That steel rod has been removed but it's left me feeling almost as hollow as I was when Grace had died.

Oh, Grace. Did I really spend twenty-three years blaming you for the way my life has turned out? God, I'm sorry, Gracie. I don't blame you. I should have listened, especially to the words you didn't say. I knew something was wrong and I didn't listen.

I guess I was holding onto my torch for too long, missing all of the shit that was hidden in the shadows. I had moved the truth away from anything that came in my spotlight, anything that could ruin my chances of building a castle of pinks. Just because they weren't in my spotlight, it didn't mean they weren't there. I'd placed them in the dark where I wasn't able to see them, but it was there, growing in the shadows like fungi—these little truths that would have made the biggest impacts on what I am now. On where I am now.

It's true what they say, that you only see what you want to see. I guess when it comes to the truth, you only see it when it's too late, when you're about to die. Because that's the only time you want to see it. That's the only time you think it matters. When really, it mattered all along, right from the beginning. At that exact moment when you chose to ignore it, that's when it mattered the most.

Irene begins to walk out of my space, leaving me here to wonder who it is that's waiting to see me. Has Patrick come to apologise? Did he escape the Crains? There's no way. Gabriel? Toni? Vin? Rossi Crain, the king himself? My circle is small and I'm running out of names. They all have a motive. This is going to be a long wait. I don't even know what fucking time it is.

I lay back and brace myself as I realise that death is approaching fast, yet I'm wondering whether it would be mine or this man here in a coma.

I wonder, do all criminals fear the dark when the end is coming? Do all criminals feel this weak before they die? Weakness has been my worst enemy since I can remember but now I need to make sure I have the strength to survive my visitor. I need a plan. Fuck. I need help.

Help. I've always needed help, even when I thought I didn't. But who asks for help anymore? Who wants to admit they can't do the things they're expected to do? Who stands there and throws their hand in the air for everyone to see? Who is there to help? *Really* help.

I don't feel good. These thoughts, they're drowning me and my head, it's throbbing. I can only thank God right now for this morphine in my blood. Maybe I deserve that at least. Maybe He feels my pain for the past thirty years. Maybe He understands why I did what I did. Maybe He realises His errors when He gave the amateur the pen to write out the story of my life. I don't know, but it seems He has sent an angel to deal with the evil spirit that's settled into my body.

But the morphine doesn't cut it. There's a whole lot more that they don't know about and only I know it's there. I need to kill that pain. I need it to go. But God, I guess He doesn't believe I'm deserving of that. Maybe He's realised, maybe He's realised that I've only been speaking to him since I've been in here, since I found out I was dying.

Stop this, Kai. Focus. You're okay. You're just tired, that's all. That's all it is. Now, think. How will you survive your visitor?

CHAPTER **TWENTY-TWO**

Truth be told

Today

I hear someone shuffling beside me. I feel my body tense up as I realise I'd fallen asleep. Someone has crept into my space and is sitting in the chair next to me. My eyes don't want to open but I can feel it, I can hear it. He is here and I don't know who *he* is. I don't know how much of the truth I want to know. I want to die. Right here, right now, I don't want to face it. I don't think I can. But I need to know they're okay, and I know *he* knows.

Light begins to creep beneath my eyelids as I open the shutter, allowing myself to see. He has come, sitting back in the chair, his body slightly tilted to a side with one leg over the other. He has a sincere look on his face as he stares at me.

'They're fine.' Gabriel speaks calmly with his voice lowered and I wonder who he thinks could be listening. But thank you, God, the girls are safe. I trust they are, I trust Gabriel. I can see it in his face, the way he's sitting. Unarmed and open.

I move my arm towards my mask. I need to speak to him but he holds up his hand to stop me and I feel like this is a common occurrence here in the hospital. I'm supposed to be muted, I'm sure they've all been ordered not to let me speak. But I don't know why. Why can't I speak?

Stop. I need to stop. I need to focus on Gabriel. Stop thinking. Stop being paranoid. Focus. Find out what's happening, find out who put you in here, Kai. Find out.

'I'd ask you how you were but I know you have questions and I know time is limited. So I'll talk. Skye and Bella, I can't get them to come here. One, because it's not safe for them, and two, because I only have Skye. Bella is missing.'

What has happened to Bella? Where is she? It's cold in here but I can feel myself sweating. I can feel the clamminess on my hands against the leather of my wallet. All I can see is Bella. Who has taken her? Wait. What do you mean you *have* Skye?

'Rest assured, they are safe and well. They're tough girls, you know?'

I know. I know they're tough, but what does this mean? How do you know she's safe? I look at his face. He's still sympathetic as he looks at me from his chair. As he looks at me and my dying state.

'I've come to bring you a message from the Crains. Your girls are safe, remember that. As long as Skye remains with me, they will be in good hands. Or at least she will.'

What? What about Bella? Where is she? Why did they separate? I don't understand. What are you telling me, Gabriel?

I stare into his eyes trying to read him like a book but his letters seem jumbled through this mask that clouds over my face. Yet somehow, he can read me.

'They are smarter than you think, Kai. You were set up, we were set up. This whole thing. My father, Toni, he's not in it for the kill. They're not after you. They're after Patrick, and the next in line, his children.' He's moving forward and now his hand is resting on my bed.

What? Next in line? What does he want with the girls? What is Toni going to do with my girls?

'Kai, listen, relax, please, he's not going to hurt them.'

Toni knew? This whole time he knew what Patrick did?

'I'm sorry you had to find out the way you did. I

didn't know either. But Dad and Vin, they knew. That's why they came after you, they scouted you before they ordered that drink in the bar. They knew you were desperate. You were in the perfect position to give them what they needed—Patrick, and his children. Rest assured, I will take care of the girls.'

What? I can't believe what I'm hearing but I do believe him. I know he's sincere. I know he's telling the truth. My chest is hurting again and I'm trying to fight it. I can't have Irene coming in to interrupt me. Not now. I need to keep calm, I need to breathe. Deep breaths. Deep breaths, Kai. Focus.

Gabriel's hand is still placed on my bed beside me. He's reaching out and I can only assume he wants my forgiveness. That, or he's going to kill me. I continue to stare at him, raising my arm slowly to take off my mask. I need to know. This isn't enough. Where is Bella? What is he doing with Skye?

'Please, the nurse told me you keep trying to take that off. Please, leave it on.' He moves his arm up and I see he's ready to move mine back down. I don't have the strength to fight.

'They needed information.' He continues to speak and I rest my arm back down by my side as my chest decides to cave in.

'Patrick had been warned off by a previous

acquaintance. The Crains worked with the owner of R.E.L many years ago, who happens to be laying in this very room. That man, right there, is Patrick's father, Ethan Healey, the owner of the biggest property chain in the country.'

Wait. Ethan? Big Ethan? The man who'd come to me for a large soy latte, Ethan? He's Patrick's dad? The one I looked at like a father? *That* Ethan? Did he pay for Grace's silence? Ethan? Ethan who came to her funeral? *He's* Patrick's dad?

I move my eyes to his bed and towards his large, strong hand as it rests by his side. Fuck.

'Kai, please. You need to remain calm and listen for a moment if you want to know what happened.'

He's right, but my head is all over the place.

'When this man dies, everything he owns will be passed down to Patrick. Except Patrick doesn't know it yet. He was never trusted to know. The Crains still have a large investment in the business and once his old man is no more, Patrick will be next in line.'

All of this, for R.E.L? That was their project, to get the twins? I still don't get it. Speak to me, Gabriel. Make me understand.

'You know, the Crains have a large share of R.E.L but there was more to it. Healey was making more money than he was letting on. He wronged them.'

I don't care. I don't care about R.E.L, I don't care about Patrick, or the fucking Crains. What are you doing with the girls? Where is Bella? I'm losing it. I can hear it. I can hear myself and I need to stop. I need to stop fucking thinking and just listen. But Bella. Where is she?

'We needed Patrick. We need those girls. I hope you understand. Patrick will die, and out of our courtesy to you, he will suffer for what he did to your Grace. I can give you my word. Skye and I will take care of R.E.L, maybe Bella too if she hands herself in. I'm sorry it turned out this way. You were never meant to end up in here.'

Maybe? Maybe Bella too? Just maybe? Skye, does she know this? Does she know what you could do to her sister? Are you keeping her from her own free will? Does she want to leave? What is going on, Gabriel? I still don't understand. This was all because of money? The past few days, I've been going out of my mind wondering what the fuck I could have done differently to not end up here and *I* was scouted? *They* came to me. *They* planned for this. Would I have had a choice? They came for me. They wanted me, of all people, it had to be me, this was supposed to be my life. This was supposed to be my death. I can't. I can't hear it, I don't want to listen. He needs to go. Fuck off, Gabriel.

He moves forward, closer to me as he places his

hand over mine. They're cold, but the words, the words coming from his mouth are on fire. Blazing like a dragon, burning through my eardrums.

'They knew what he did to your sister, Kai. To all of those other girls. This scum right here protected Patrick as soon as he found out what he did to Grace. We needed your help and you were magnificent at it. This business is worth billions of pounds. We're all set to take down R.E.L but your information led us to something else. Healey had thousands of warehouses across England working on a secret operation that the Crains had sussed out using the additional information you'd taken from Patrick. Locations, names, and business procedures. He was crucial to this last step. He had no idea what he was giving away. If that old man had trusted him more, Patrick may have been more reluctant to tell you some of the things he did.'

Shut up. Just shut up, Gabriel. Shut up for one second, let me just… I can't believe this. Ethan, you knew? You knew your son raped my sister? You knew why Gracie died, and you came to me, every fucking day, to listen to me cry over coffee?

'Those warehouses, they're used to store heroin, Kai. As soon as this man becomes nothing but a corpse, billions of pounds worth of drugs will be pumped out into the streets of England and it will all belong to Skye and Bella.'

I'm numb. I wanted to give them all the money in the world and now they have it. They have everything made for them. Except their money is being made from producing the same thing that killed their mother. Did I seriously just do this? Did I just help the Crains take ownership of a massive operation to get more drugs out onto the streets when it could have died with Ethan? It was the very thing that killed my sister, the very thing that got me stuck into this mess.

I can see a layer of mist glaze over Gabriel's eyes and they don't seem so sincere anymore. Just kill me already.

'We set you up, Kai. And you took the bait.' He moves back to sit comfortably in his chair again.

What do you mean, 'we'? You said you didn't know? How much can I trust you, Gabriel?

'Toni has personally asked me to tell you that Patrick will pay for what he did to your sister. You did everything according to the plan and for that, you will not be punished. But I can't say the same for Bella.'

What!? No, not Bella. What did she do? How was she involved in this at all? I jolt my arm up and grab hold of my mask and tug on it. You don't touch Bella. You don't hurt her. The sound of air gushes out through the sides of my mask. My chest tightens up and my muscles feel as though they're contracting. I can feel it. Death. It hurts, my chest hurts, my ribs, my back, everything. I'm trying to speak but I can't. My mouth is numb and the words I'm trying to say leave as muffled sounds and I realise I'm slurring.

'Kai, please. Just listen.' Gabriel leans forward again and begins to tighten my mask back on to my face but it's too late. I've realised. I've realised I can breathe fine without it. What were they pumping into me? What the fuck is happening? Why can't I speak?

'I told the girls that night you were in the garage. I told them that Patrick is their father. They didn't give me a chance to explain. Bella was furious that you hid it from her. There was no talking to her. We tried to explain and calm her down but she was out of control and she left. Toni and Vin are looking for her. They will find her and she will face the wrath.'

Wrath for what? Running away? Wanting to be by herself? Did she kill Patrick? Oh, Bella, no.

'Kai, please, listen. Skye knows everything. I told her and she is working with me now. It's the only way I can keep her safe. But Bella? This bee, she stings. We still needed you for Patrick. But this bee stuck her stinger right through your chest and messed the whole thing up. But don't worry. What happens to a bee when she stings?'

221

Bella. Bella drove a stake through my chest? My Bella? No. I did everything for them. There was no way, not even the slightest. She would never do that, not to me. No. Fuck off, Gabriel. Fuck off.

I'm losing it again. I'm burning up and that machine, it's going off screeching through me as though a hundred steel shafts are being impaled into me at one time. What the fuck is this? Stop. Stop. Just fuck off, Gabriel. Bella would never hurt me. Where is Irene? Why isn't she coming?

'Kai, please, calm down. I'm trying to tell you.'

He gets up from the chair and plays around with the machine behind me.

'Mr Jackson?'

Thank God, Irene. Get this man out of here.

'It's okay, Nurse. I've got this.' Gabriel gives her a stern look and she walks away. Whatever he's done, it's stabilised my breathing. At least for now.

He's sitting back down. The silence between us makes me realise I need him to speak. I do need to know. Fucking say something, Gabriel.

'We came to you that night, Kai. But she got there first. Skye and I, we tried to stop her. You taught them well. About family. But Bella thinks Patrick is her family. She doesn't know the truth, she doesn't know about Grace or the other girls. All she knows is that you kept her father a secret from her. She thinks you knew the entire time, and she only sees that you tried to kill him.'

I don't know how I'm supposed to feel right now, but fuck! Bella, I would never harm you. Why did you do it? You tried to *kill* me. And now I'm here. I'm still here, waiting to die. But, inside, you've already killed me. God, Bella. Why?

'We need her on our side, Kai, or she may have to go. This business will not work if it's split between two sisters with different agendas.'

I can feel my tears as they travel around the edges of my mask, dancing in front of me, mocking me as the airflow pushes them around my face. I need you to leave now Gabriel. I need to be alone.

'You did good by us, Kai. Toni thought you deserved the truth.'

I can finally see the Crains for who they are. A group of criminals who hire people to kill for them because of the power that they gained from the digits in their bank accounts. It was a business that ran under the name of 'Family' funded by their inheritance. 'Family' was just a word with no real meaning except to entice people like me. Those who were desperate for cash and on the fight for survival. Those like me who were right at the bottom of the ladder, so far down that even the first rung was impossible to step onto. Those lost souls in need of a family. In need of support. That's how they found us. That's how they found me. Not by chance, but through observation and a lot of conversations. Networking. Building bridges between people, only to burn them later on.

'I tried to hang on until we found Bella, to give you better news, but Nurse Ivanova advised me to come sooner.'

Nurse Ivanova, the angel of death, I knew it.

'You did good, Kai. Farewell soldier.'

I place the cover over my lenses and embrace the darkness.

CHAPTER **TWENTY-THREE**

That's the beauty of dying

Now

The softness beneath my fingers soothes me as I run them along the intricate pattern that's stitched into the leather of my wallet. I can't help but allow for it to appease me. Since when did my desire for things give me a feeling of peace and happiness? Happiness. What is that?

The journey to happiness is a sad path to walk along. I spent my life searching for this feeling of contentment rather than *being*. I picked up a lot of clutter along the way that made me feel as though it would bring me joy. It was the devil's way of luring me in, using it to dictate my lifestyle. I thought it was bringing me happiness but it was a trick. A trick to get me close. Maybe it was an illusion, like hope and death. It was the devil's game. It was a scam and he already had me. He had me from the moment I stepped onto that path, when I felt like I needed more than what I already had.

All those things I bought, all those distractions, they only delivered an illusion of happiness because beneath all of those things I had owned, was a man, a weak man drowning in grief. Maybe I still am. I don't know.

With a flick of a switch, it all turns to darkness. It kisses my skin and whispers through my ears. It's my favourite place to be, the darkness. But I'm ready to step into the light.

We don't realise how fast he creeps upon us. This thing called death. He'll come for all of us and he doesn't discriminate. Good, bad, right, wrong, it doesn't matter. He pays no attention to who you are, how much you have or what you have done. He favours no one. No one will leave this world alive. Death. It's inevitable.

As for life, I don't understand it. I don't know the meaning of it and I don't know why we spend most of ours trying to find out. Although I do know that it's not about things.

I've never had as much money as I do right now, but this is the poorest I've ever been. Money doesn't make a person rich. People do. And it's taken for me to die to understand that. We spend our lives fighting to survive knowing we're going to die anyway. The more I try to understand it, the more fucked up it seems.

Bad things happen to people, no matter how good or bad they are. What makes a person bad? What makes a person good? Who decides what's considered good or bad? What are the boundaries? None of it matters when you're dead. None of it matters. All that matters is what's left with you when you go. What's left of you when you go. What stays with you. The person you are. The people you're with. The memories you leave behind.

I close my eyes as the scent of strawberry jam fills my nostrils. Grace looks up and smiles at me as she rips her piece of bread in half and hands it over to me. I'm smiling too as I look over at Mum as she watches us eat the food that she put on the table. That *she* put on the table.

I understand now. The responsibility was never given to me, I'd taken it, following the rules of society, hanging on to it tightly without sharing it.

I understand now. The art of letting go paints a beautiful masterpiece and I wish I'd held on to that paintbrush a long time ago.

I understand now. I take my last breaths as I

finally get it. Life. It's not just about living. It's about loving. Leaving this world, dying with those you love around you, because that's all I want right now, Skye and Bella, Mum and Grace. All I want is to be surrounded by their warmth. Not money or things, not what I've done or what I could have done. It's dying in peace, spending my last days with the people I love.

I wish they were here with me, but they're not.

ACKNOWLEDGEMENTS

When it came to getting into the mindset of my characters, I found it challenging writing about their depression, anxiety and suicide. There were many times whilst researching and writing *Seven Sins*, where I wanted to give up and stop because of how I felt during the process. So I have to thank everyone who encouraged me to keep going.

Thank you to my parents Prabha and Narendra Manani, who will always be on the top of my acknowledgement and gratitude lists. I can't thank you enough for your continuous support in every decision I've made throughout my entire life.

I'm genuinely thankful for each of my beta readers who used so much of their own time to support me. Amarpreet Kaur Sohal, I seriously don't know how you managed to squeeze this into your busy schedule with three little kids and your beautiful cake business, and not just once either. Your honest feedback genuinely transformed this novel, so thank you. Robert Harrison, thank you for also taking time out from your busy schedule to read *Seven Sins* on multiple occasions, especially when you were writing the third novel in your Onyx trilogy. There is a huge difference throughout all of my revisions thanks to your extensive feedback. Jaimen Maisuria, I still cannot believe you took a day off work to read this in one sitting – thank you for doing that and thank you for your honest feedback and suggestions on how I could make this novel better. Amar, Robert, Jaimen, you have been awesome beta readers and I'm genuinely thankful to all of you for your support, motivation and comments!

Stacey Dee, thank you for sharing your knowledge of gang crime and criminal psychology. It made me realise how I'd been living in a bubble in thinking that the mafia and the likes of were just myths… oops.

Nurse Ruth Ayres, where do I start? I was overwhelmed by the amount of support you gave me in ensuring I understood the processes and procedures for someone in Kai's situation. Your knowledge and passion for what you do is truly amazing and selfless. I genuinely appreciate the amount of care that goes into looking after a patient, especially one you know will not make it. I was, and still am, overwhelmed by the extensive amount of care that goes into looking after someone who is dying.

Nurse Ruth Ayres currently works as a Lung Cancer Macmillan Nurse in London, England and had originally trained and qualified in Australia. She has specialised in Palliative Care and Oncology and loves nursing. If there is anything unrealistic about the level of care or experiences faced by the characters in this novel, please note it was intentional and does not reflect on the accuracy of the advice and information Ruth has provided.

Thank you, Michelle Young, author of the psychological thrillers *Your Move*, and *There She Lies*. Michelle has truly inspired and motivated me throughout the entire process, sharing so much of her positive energy and excitement along the way.

Kelly Brady Channick, YA author of the *Asbury High* cosy mystery series, shared her insight with me into the planning process of her novels. She doesn't know it yet but because of her information, I was able to conjure up and plan a little more into Book 2 of the *Seven* series, which originally wasn't going to be a series. So thank you, Kelly. It was so good to wind down and escape into *Asbury High and the Parcels of Poison* after I'd written so much darkness in *Seven Sins*.

Robert Harrison, the author of *The Onyx Trilogy*, also one of my beta readers and master editor behind *Seven Sins*, thank you for the ongoing motivation, enthusiasm and feedback from reading the first chapter of the first draft of *Seven Sins*, to the final version and the ones in between.

Prashant Chavda, thank you for your efforts in sourcing beta readers, and for running around with the printing – I really do appreciate it.

Sinth Siva, I love the new character names you came up with for *Seven Sins* compared to what I had - thank you for encouraging me to change them.

Mayuri Sachin Taylor, thank you for constantly pushing me, motivating me, lifting me and still sharing that continuous level of excitement and positive energy with me. I can't express the level of gratitude I have for you.

My sister, Nisha, the same goes for you. Even though you're not an avid reader, thank you for sharing every single one of my posts on social media and for listening to my constant updates about what I'm writing about. I hope one day you'll read one of my books, or *a* book – it doesn't even have to be mine!

My niece, Shreya, thank you for asking me how my book was going every other day and smiling at me on the days I told you it wasn't going well. And thank you for not telling me to start again ;)

And of course, a huge thank you to everyone who had supported me with my first novel, *The Colours of Denial*. You gave me the encouragement, motivation and confidence through your positive energy, feedback and reviews, and because of that, I was able to write *Seven Sins*.

Thank you. Once again, sending high-fives, hearts and smiley face emoji's to you all.

A THANK YOU FROM ARTI

Thank you for reading *Seven Sins*. As a new, independent author, knowing that you chose to read this book amongst billions of others means a great deal to me and I am hugely thankful to you.

I don't want to stop at a *thank you* - I'd love to engage with you. I'd love to hear about the kind of books you like to read, what you do in your spare time and what you think about *Seven Sins*. I'd love to know if it has affected you in any way, if you'd like to see more novels like this from me, or even if it wasn't for you. Why? Because feedback plays a huge part when it comes to improvement – and I'm all for that.

It also plays a massive part when it comes to exposure. If you enjoyed reading *Seven Sins*, I would love it if you could help spread the word. Be it through word of mouth, leaving a review on Amazon or Goodreads, or even contacting me on the channels below, I'd truly appreciate it.

Instagram: @Author_Arti_Manani
Facebook: AuthorArtiManani
Email: AuthorArtiManani@hotmail.com

If you'd like to be the first to hear about my bookish updates, email me using the address above with *Mailing List – SS* as your subject line.
In the meantime, read on for chapter one from my debut novel, *The Colours of Denial.*

WHEN THE ONLY WAY OUT
IS TO FACE THE TRUTH

THE **COLOURS** OF
DENIAL

ARTI MANANI

CHAPTER **ONE**

The man with the blurred face is getting closer. She's increased her pace but beneath her feet, the sharp grains of sand blackened by the darkness pulls her down into the ground, working her harder to leave the shadows. The clouds have encroached across the moon and the desert is dim, leaving her with no company other than the figures created inside her head. Her heart is pumping against her chest, with each beat louder than the one before and each breath heavier, as she comes to realise that she may not get away. Away from the darkness, the shadows and this unknown man with the blurred face. Her legs are weak and heavy and she begins to slow down until eventually, she stops running, accepting her defeat. The sun will soon rise, threatening to expose her. She has nowhere to hide.

The sound of breathlessness fades as her heart slows. Light appears in the distance as the sun gently pushes its way through the blackness. She stands, as she witnesses this miraculous fight between light and dark. The sun, so powerful that not even the shadows can defeat it, begins to celebrate its victory by showing off its vibrant, fiery colours across the skies, sprinkling the desert with gold dust. Even the clouds have surrendered and in this moment, she is calm. The world is still and silent. She stands motionless, feeling content. She is embraced by the sun's heat. Safe. Warm. The man with the blurred face has disappeared.

***

Sunday, 17 September 2017, 4:45 a.m. The curtains were drawn but the dim light from the streetlamp outside her window came flooding in, casting dark, creepy figures across the room. Sophia lay in bed, tucked beneath her thick duvet staring at the ceiling, recalling her latest nightmare. The man was getting closer. A drop of sweat trickled from her forehead and down the side of her face. It was only a matter of time until she would fall asleep, and it was only a matter of time until she would be face to face with this mysterious man who had been watching her, following her, haunting her in her dreams.

She turned her body and glanced over at Oliver as he slept beside her. His long, curly, brown hair swept across his face as he lay there, peacefully. She wanted to wake him from his sleep, to talk to him, to tell him about her nightmare. She wanted him to comfort her and tell her she was safe. But he was asleep, snoring gently beside her, calm and still. A deep sigh of disappointment escaped from her mouth as she disregarded the thought of waking him, slowly turning to move into her original position. She lay on her back once again, lost in her duvet, wide awake as she stared at the blank ceiling.

Cold sweat continued to seep from her pores as her mind became hazy, clouded by the happenings of her recent nightmares. She was unable to forget, no matter how hard she tried. A secured box that was buried deep inside her was forcing itself open, compelling her to recall some of her previous encounters with the man with the blurred face. The danger wasn't real, but she was terrified. She lay there, trying to stay afloat in a pool of memories that were weighing her down, and drowning her in her own thoughts. It didn't matter that Oliver had been sleeping beside her. Sophia felt alone as she suffocated in the silence that surrounded her. It was the same silence which would later be interrupted by all of the nasty voices inside her head, as they constantly reminded her that she was not alone.

Sophia's eyes were heavy and tired but she refused to give her body what it was asking for. She refused to let herself fall asleep or rest, in fear of being tormented by another nightmare. The man with the blurred face had been getting too close, too fast.

She wasn't ready. She clenched on to her duvet as she pulled it up, tucking it under her chin, covering her body as if the duvet was a shield against her fears. She moved her arms beneath the covers, resting them by her sides as she lay there still, quiet and afraid as her armour failed to do the job she intended it to.

The voices inside her head had awakened from their peace as they hissed in a whisper through her ears. They slithered inside Sophia's mind and through her thoughts, entrancing her under a spell of anxiety, spilling all of her worries that she had stored away. Her dark thoughts spilled like a large coffee overflowing in an espresso cup. The coffee was bitter and strong, full of caffeine. It was a drug she didn't like, an addiction of darkness that was embedded inside her. It was a coffee being served without a smile, and one that she didn't want to drink.

The voices inside her head would strike her

often, forcing open a box of instincts, gut feelings, and signs that she had ignored and buried within. Yet no matter how far down it was hidden, the truth remained on the surface of her soul and the voices would be sure to remind her.

The voices continued to hiss at her as the drums of her heartbeat throbbed through her ears. She began to fight the snakes inside her, pushing the lid back onto the box, forcing it down. She lay there, breathing deeply while releasing some of her nicer thoughts as they soaked up the bitterness of the spilt coffee like a sponge. She lay there, trying to recreate the safe zone that had once existed.

Her bed was a place of security, where she could escape and lock herself away and be free. It was her hiding place. A place to run away where no-one would disturb her. It was the place where she could be herself, weak and sensitive, without the need to pretend that she was anything else. But the safe zone was no more, the voices inside her head told her so. Safety had become a distant memory and her safe zone was transformed into a place surrounded by dark and evil thoughts. It had become a place where she'd have many sleepless nights where she'd force herself to stay awake with no choice but to listen to the torturous voices inside her head. It had become a place where she would eventually fall asleep and be tormented in her nightmares. Her bed had become a place where she could no longer run or hide.

She turned around, grabbing on to what was left of her consciousness as she slipped out from beneath the duvet, snuggling her feet into her navy blue slipper boots. It was cold on the other side of the duvet, cold and gloomy. But she was better off.

Sophia tiptoed over to the silhouette of her overly busy dressing table, quietly, trying not to wake up Oliver. She picked up her hairbrush from its assigned area, nudging a jewellery box out of the way at the same time. Bad move. The box pushed a bottle of Chanel perfume off the table and she jolted her left arm forward to save it from smashing against the wooden interior of their bedroom floor. Saved. But a slight touch of her elbow to a can of hair spray sent it tumbling to the floor. It was dark after-all and inevitable given the state of her dressing table. The hair spray was not hers and had no assigned place on this table. If Oliver were to wake up now, it was his own doing. But he didn't flinch, oblivious to his surroundings.

Sophia began to comb her hair - fine and golden like the desert sands that haunted her in her sleep, each strand glowing like the rays of sun that had been threatening to expose her to the dark shadows and the man with the blurred face. The hair spray rolled towards Oliver's abandoned exercise bike near the window, which now served the purpose of being a dumping ground for clothes. She glanced over at him. Despite the noise, he didn't move. He lay still, fast asleep, peacefully.

'Sorry,' she apologised in a whisper. 'About to head out for a jog.' Sophia put the hairbrush back in its allocated spot, ignoring the hair spray on the floor. She grabbed her running clothes that had been hanging from the handlebars of the exercise bike, before leaving the room.

She switched on the light as she entered the bathroom and stood at the basin, squinting and blinking as her eyes readjusted to the brightness of the large, round, moon-like ceiling light. She stared at her reflection in a small, oval mirror which sat on a little shelf above the sink. The mirror had a blue and green mosaic tile border around it. Some of the tiles were missing and the mirror itself had a chip not too far off from the centre. Despite its current state, she held on to it.

Sophia smiled at her reflection, staring at herself beyond the cracks and chips. She looked strong and controlled, independent, powerful, feisty, confident. She looked like everything she was not. She stood out, like a lion in a field of green, living in an environment that wasn't made for her, where she was always seen, but made to hide. The shades of golds and browns in her hair, the shape and depth of her large, orangey-brown eyes, and her buttoned nose were very much like the features of a lion. She played a perfectly good role in holding up the appearance of being strong and courageous, but she hid the real animal inside her, always afraid, always looking out for danger, always running away - Sophia, the meerkat.

She turned on the tap and began to wash away the sweat from her face as the ice-cold water began to steal her warmth. She changed into her black leggings and Oliver's baggy sweatshirt and stood there, soothed by the scent of his Armani aftershave as she closed her eyes and held her breath. The scent filled her with gratitude and awe as she reconnected with herself, embracing the steadiness of her soul with Oliver's. She exhaled slowly as she looked into the mirror proudly before turning to exit the bathroom.

Sophia headed down the stairs, quietly, slipping her feet out of her navy blue slipper boots, and into her black and orange trainers, stuffing bits of her mane into a bun at the same time.

The front door instantly slammed shut behind her. She jumped as the sound echoed through her ears, spilling more coffee from the overflowing cup inside her head. Flashbacks of the nightmare from nearly seven months ago came back to haunt her, when the man with a blurred face first came knocking on her door.

'No,' Sophia whispered to herself as she turned away from the house. She jogged down the steps and onto the street, telling herself that she was not going to be afraid, even though she was.

It was around 5:30 in the morning. The street was cold and eerie with little life other than that of the handful of other lone joggers and dog walkers. Sophia began to jog down the pavement. She jogged along three blocks, past houses, a petrol station, a church and her old high school, before she reached the entrance of her local park. She dodged out of the way of an elderly man who was walking out with his old and sad looking golden retriever. The dog immediately began to bark at her, angry and ferocious like a raging fire.

'Sorry,' Sophia apologised under her breath as she looked down at the ground, ashamed and afraid, avoiding any eye contact with this stranger and his dog. The dog continued to bark viciously at her for coming too close to his master as she scurried, moving further away from them and from any confrontation that could have come of it. The old man ignored her but the dog's barking was persistent as it growled angrily at Sophia, threatening her with its sharp, claw-like teeth. The man had been trying to pull at the dogs' leash, embarrassed and keen to keep walking.

She jogged through the gates of the park and stopped at a bench just inside the entrance to tighten her laces, skimming around at the same time to see if anyone else was there. As usual, like any other Sunday morning, not one single being was to be seen. Three empty cans of Budweiser were stood on the floor beside the bench, making her wary as she looked around, cautious and paranoid in case the culprit was still hanging around. Nobody was there.

Sophia began to jog down a wide path with mountains of golden brown leaves that had been swept to the sides. The park was beautiful and came to life with the vibrant colours of autumn. Trees stood tall and proud every two meters down the path on both the left and right of her. The fields behind them were spotted with evergreen bushes and more trees holding on to what they had left of their red and gold leaves. It was perfection at its finest.

The whole park was the most peaceful and positive place to be in and the perfect place for Sophia to escape. Escape from all of her problems, her nightmares, reality. Everything would disappear, except the voices inside her head as they continued to abuse the drugs from the overflowing coffee cup, addicted to the demonic energy being served within.

Sophia jogged along a sandy footpath that went through a woodland area of tall trees, long grass and bushy hedges.

'Get away.' 'Get out.' 'Go.' The voices inside Sophia's head began to mutter, getting louder and sharper like an angry and violent windstorm. She ignored the tornado that was beginning to form inside her and jogged past a children's playground area, and up a hilly slope that sat further away from the playground, overlooking the nicer part of town.

'You did this, Sophia.' The howling inside her head began to turn into a storm, forming angry flashes of lightning into her soul, creating a burning fire within. But she took no notice, she was nearly there. She jogged down the hill and approached a large pond with a fountain in the middle that sat at the end of the park, not too far from the hilly slope. Opposite the pond was Lilly's, a small and cosy café hidden deep inside the park. She continued to jog around the pond, slowing down her pace as the sounds of the fountain sprinkled into her ears. She was there. The sounds began to drown out the voices that had been hissing at her from inside her head, extinguishing the fire that had been created by the intensity of the caffeine-induced storm. There was something about the sound of running water that made Sophia feel at peace. It surrounded her with a sense of harmony giving her the warm hug that she'd been yearning for. She was exhausted. She was tired of running in the park, in her sleep, away from everything throughout her entire life. But she needed this run, it was one with a purpose. A purpose she was yet to figure out.

Just over an hour had passed and Sophia had run over fifteen laps around the park before she decided to head back home. She'd been running almost every day for nearly seven months, but fifteen laps was a new accomplishment for her. Yet she didn't feel a sense of achievement. The closer the man with the blurred face got to her in her nightmares, the more laps around the park she would do out of fear and panic, running away from her problems and the negativity that came with it. Fifteen laps wasn't something to be proud of, it was a sign of failure. Her failure.

Sophia walked, slowly and out of breath towards the same gates that she had entered through. Puffs of condensation left her mouth as she exhaled. She wanted to get back into bed. She was tired, drained and in need of rest but she couldn't let herself fall asleep. She knew the impact of drifting off, she couldn't risk it. Wrestling against tiredness to stay awake and being tortured by the voices inside her head were far more appealing than the effects of falling asleep.

As she walked closer towards the exit, a sudden

feeling of uneasiness filled her gut. Everything seemed off and the air had become colder and bitter. A sudden gust of wind struck her face startling the voices inside her head as they began to scream. The sounds tore through her skin like shards of glass being thrown at her in masses. Sophia stopped dead in her tracks. She stood there, terrified and numb. Someone was there, watching her. The figure sat in the distance, on the bench where she'd tightened her laces. He sat, in his muddy blue jeans and his unzipped, dark brown bomber jacket over a navy blue hoodie. His face was down but his eyes were on her, staring at her, watching her.

Uncomfortable, confused and scared, Sophia was loyal to her fears. She froze as her brain refused to communicate with the rest of her body. Her legs became heavy and her meerkat survival tactic had failed her before she could even attempt to run. She kept her eyes on this figure. He was observing her, watching her. The fine hairs on the back of her neck rose as terror struck her soul. Her muscles became tense. She wanted to run but had become paralysed to the spot. The voices inside her head screamed at her to move but she remained stationary. Her mind became clouded with fear. There was nothing she could do. Sophia was weak. He watched her as she stood there, trying to fight the battle with herself.

Adrenaline activated her nervous system as the sound of her heart pounding into her ears became louder and louder. Her blood began to pump through her body viciously bringing her back from her numbness. The man was still watching. It was fight or flight. The voices inside her head began to panic, awakening her meerkat instincts – flight. She began to move, scurrying to the side making sure there was going to be enough space between herself and this man. She had to pass him to get out of the park, she had to be quick, she had to escape. Her legs were heavy as a strong magnetic force began to pull them down towards the ground, making it harder for her to get away. The happenings of her nightmares were becoming real. Her paranoia kicked in and she panicked.

'Who is he?' 'Why is he here?' 'What does he want?' The voices inside her head began to scream at her all at once. 'This is your fault, Sophia.' 'Why are you running?' 'You'll be dead soon.' The nastiness of the voices terrified her. They screamed suddenly with no warning, biting away chunks of her soul each time, making her feel unsafe and unstable in her own body. She sped up, trying to get away from the man, from the voices, from herself. Her large, lion-like eyes filled with fear as she continued to feel his eyes piercing through her skin. She couldn't see his face, she didn't look long enough, hard enough. Her goal, for that moment, was to get out of the park, alive. She was a few meters from the gate, but so was he. Sophia sped up and with each step and each skip of her heartbeat, found herself running. She could see him, from the side of her eye as he began to rise from the bench, slowly, face down, eyes still on her.

'Shit!' she whispered to herself as her heart pumped rapidly inside her chest. The meerkat scurried, heading towards the gates, towards this man, hoping she'd get there first.

'Yo!'

A voice called from behind her but she wasn't going to stop. It wasn't real, it wasn't happening, no-one was going to save her. Sophia knew only she could save herself. She wished someone was there to help her, but it wasn't real. She continued to run convincing herself that there was no-one there to help, that it was the voices inside her head, that it was all her imagination. But the man was still there, walking forwards, watching her, waiting.

She ran, away from the voice, away from this strange man, and out of the park gates. She ran down the street with her heart still pumping recklessly. She ran until she was at a safe distance, away from the park, until she was ready to slow down. Still nervous and scared, Sophia turned around. Her entire body was numb with fear. The man was gone. Sophia had escaped, just like in her nightmares. But she hadn't won, and she knew it. This man was still hunting her, teasing her, preparing to move in. Did her nightmare just become real? Sophia was screwed. Whether she was awake or asleep, he was there, and there was nothing she could do. She scurried home. Sophia, the meerkat.

THE **COLOURS** OF
DENIAL

ARTI MANANI

Manufactured by Amazon.ca
Bolton, ON